HANNAH AND HAWK

Hometown Love Book Two

MEGAN MCCOY

Published by Blushing Books
An Imprint of
ABCD Graphics and Design, Inc.
A Virginia Corporation
977 Seminole Trail #233
Charlottesville, VA 22901

©2019
All rights reserved.

No part of the book may be reproduced or transmitted in any form or by any means, electronic or mechanical, including photocopying, recording, or by any information storage and retrieval system, without permission in writing from the publisher. The trademark Blushing Books is pending in the US Patent and Trademark Office.

Megan McCoy
Hannah and Hawk

EBook ISBN: 978-1-64563-141-5
Print ISBN: 978-1-64563-218-4

Cover Art by ABCD Graphics & Design
This book contains fantasy themes appropriate for mature readers only. Nothing in this book should be interpreted as Blushing Books' or the author's advocating any non-consensual sexual activity.

Chapter 1

Hannah Koberline rolled her eyes and laughed at her brother Hunter as he unlocked the door to their hardware store. "What do you mean, you hate truck day? What kind of attitude is that? Lots of new things to put on the shelf and make us some money."

"It's 4 a.m.," he complained. "I closed last night."

"We close at 7 p.m.," she reminded him. "But yeah, I know you didn't get out of here until late. It looks great." She looked around the dark store as they headed back to the storage room. It had been six months since they bought it and moved here from St. Peters, MO. She enjoyed southern Illinois, adored Macintyre and really loved her store. She wasn't crazy about having to share it with her sometimes bossy big brother, but it worked out generally, and they mostly worked well together. They should, they'd had lots of practice at it. She and Hunter had been working together since they were children, so while he was annoying, she was used to him. Looking for a house and getting out of the studio apartment was next on her list, now that they had some good people hired and her schedule settled down to something manageable. Sure, it would be the holidays soon, and those were always crazy busy during retail sales, but nothing she couldn't handle.

She and Hunter had grown up in their dad's hardware store, both working there as soon as they could walk, and she'd always dreamed of taking it over after he retired. A few years ago, while she had been away, a junior at college, Hunter, who was three years older, had shown up at her dorm room. He'd graduated from the same college a few years earlier, and had gone back to work in the store, just like she thought she would. When he told her that their dad had lost the store through a combination of medical debts for their cancer-stricken mom, and gambling debts that he ran up trying to pay off those bills, she'd been devastated. For her parents, of course, but also for Hunter and for herself. All their dreams, all their plans, just gone. Her folks had moved to Florida and moved in with her grandmother not long after that.

She finished her degree in business administration and went to work in an insurance office and had been miserable. One day while surfing on the net, dreaming, she'd run across this little hardware store for sale in a place called Macintyre, Illinois. She'd never heard of it, but started researching, went to visit that weekend and just fell in love with it. Both the town and the store which was just off the thriving main street downtown and apparently a destination point. There was a big box store at the edge of town, but looking at Mr. Jordan's numbers, she'd been impressed. She approached Hunter who was unhappily running a grocery store, and between the two of them, they'd managed financing and moved to Macintyre.

"Hey, Rodney," she said to the man standing outside the back door when she rolled it up.

"Morning, Hannah, Hunter," he replied. Rodney had worked there for Mr. Jordan and was the only one of his employees who stayed when they bought it. He only worked a few days a week but was an invaluable help and a wealth of knowledge on both store practices and town issues. He was mostly retired and she really appreciated him coming in to give them support, at least during start up.

"Truck is on time this morning," he said. "Just talked to Tristan."

Rodney knew all the drivers, all the sales reps and all the merchandisers, and almost everyone in town it seemed. Of course, he'd been there since the store first opened over three decades ago.

"Good deal," Hannah said, flipping on the lights in the stock room as he came in. "Hunter will be glad to get out of here early today. I hope Jer shows up on time."

"He will," Rodney said. "He's a good worker. I know his family."

Hannah agreed with him, silently. They had hired some very good people, including Jer who was attending community college nearby and his dad was some kind of contractor, so he knew the business.

She loved working in the store, but was glad that she had mostly decent hours now. They were open six days a week, which felt odd to her, but most of downtown here in Macintyre closed on Sunday and she and Hunter had decided to keep up that tradition, at least for now. That could change at some point, probably over the holidays, but right now, it was nice to have a known day off, just like what she called real people. Real people hours! She opened three days, and closed two days and so Hunter did the opposite, then Rodney opened once and closed once a week so they could have another day off a week. She often worked hers, doing planograms or cleaning shelves, or whatever, but that was her choice and not something she'd ask anyone else to do. Hunter liked to leave for the lake as soon as he got a day off. He was just boat crazy and worked to support his hobby. She was store crazy and worked because she loved it.

Hearing the buzzer at the front door, she went back through the dark store to let Jer in, and lock it behind him. "Good morning," she said to the lanky young man. Jer worked here about twenty hours a week. He learned quickly, and thanks to his dad, seemed to know a lot about hardware, electrical and customer service. A big thing for a nineteen-year-old to have. She'd been impressed. His folks must be great.

"Morning," he said. "Brought everyone a biscuit." He handed her a bag and she smelled something wonderful.

"Your dad make them?" she asked, opening it. Jer's dad seemed to have amazing skills in just about everything.

"This morning," he said. "Help yourself, he fed me already."

"I think I love your dad," she said, biting into the flaky warm biscuit smothered in honey butter.

Jer rolled his eyes. "I'll be sure and tell Hawk that. He'll be thrilled."

"You call your dad by your last name?" she asked. That was odd. Wasn't it?

"Yeah, everyone does," he said and headed to the stock room while she followed at a slower place, enjoying her biscuit and the quietness of the store. Soon the truck would be here and things would be crazy for a few hours before they opened at eight. Then she'd be stocking shelves and helping customers and overseeing the cashiers the rest of the day. Man, this was a good biscuit. She needed the recipe. She needed to unload the truck.

A few hours later, she looked into the eyes of the most handsome man she'd ever seen. A Matthey McConaughey clone? Maybe? Gray eyes. Dark hair with barely visible silver streaks. Scruffy beard, six-foot-tall, at least, she could see his muscles, and well, he was luscious.

"Hello, you must be Hannah. I'm Derrick Hawk. My boy Jer works here and I came to bring him his schoolbooks he left on the counter this morning."

Hannah tried to make her mouth work or her brain. Either one. This man. Well, he was old – probably ten years older than she was. Who cared? Umm, whatever. Books. He brought books. Jer and Hunter were still in the back room, sorting stock, she'd just unlocked the door for customers and he had been waiting outside for her. No, for Jer. For books? Derrick. Or Hawk. Wow.

"Biscuits," she said. Oh wow, again. That was intelligent.

"You liked them?" He smiled at her and her knees buckled. No, they didn't. They just trembled a little.

"I did. Thank you," she managed. See, she was smart and words came out of her mouth that made sense.

"Homegrown honey," he said, and she tried not to swoon. Honey. Oh, yeah, bees. Did she like bees? Oh, yeah, she freaking loved bees. What was going on in her head?

"I'm Hannah," she said.

He grinned at her and her breath caught. "I thought you were Hannah," he said as if he hadn't realized that when he walked in and she was an idiot and now what did she say?

"I loved the honey." Yeah, now he knew she was an idiot. So she added, "And the biscuit. Thank you."

"I'm glad," he said and put three books on the checkout lane. "Will you make sure Jer gets these? I'm so proud of that boy."

"Me, too," she said as if that were a thing. Yeah, she was proud of the kid who helped unload the truck. Of course she was. Why wouldn't she be?

He laughed, and said, "Well, Hannah, it was good to meet you. I'll be heading to work now. If you ever need something in your house or store fixed, give me a call, okay?" With that he put down a business card on the counter and walked back out the door.

Her stomach flip-flopped and her knees shook. What had just happened? She watched him walk out the door to a huge green pickup truck in the lot. Green was her new favorite color. Watching him drive away, she wondered what was wrong with her. What had just happened? Lightning bolt? Idiocy? That man was amazing. Nothing more, nothing less. She had never had someone affect her like that before. Never. Good thing he left because she had work to do. Would she have been able to work if he stayed? She didn't really think so, because the truck had driven away and she was still staring at where it was in the parking lot.

"Hi, Tonya," she said as the morning cashier finally walked in. Hannah felt like hugging her. If Tonya had been on time, she would have been in the back room sorting stock and not unlocking the door and meeting... well, him. Him.

"Sorry, I'm late," Tonya said. "Overslept." Stashing her purse under the counter, she opened the drawer to count the money.

"No worries," Hannah said. "Not had any customers yet. I'll go get you some candy to stock. Those are Jer's books on the counter. His dad brought them in."

"Oh man, I missed Hawk? Serves me right for being late. The man is fine, isn't he?"

"He is," Hannah agreed feeling a twinge of something that could not be jealousy. What could she possibly be jealous of? Nothing. Shaking her head, she headed to the back room to grab some boxes and get to work.

"Good morning," she looked up a few hours later to see Jess, who had been in here a few times, getting things for her new house. They had hit it off right away.

"Hi, Jess," Hannah smiled at her. She hadn't made many friends here in town yet between work, and work, and then working some more, but Jess was always friendly when she came in. She was a teacher here in town, and had been recently married. "Hi, Sam," she greeted the little boy with her.

Sam held out his arms to her. He was the friendliest little fellow and gave the best hugs. Swooping him up, she hugged him, then put him down. "He's a doll."

"I know. How lucky am I?" Jess said. "Hey, I dropped by to give you an invite. I'm having some girlfriends over this evening for," she air-quoted, "book club." Laughing, she picked up Sam who had started pulling things off the shelf. "We call it book club, but it's really us sitting around having some wine and talking. I know you haven't been in town long and it might be a good way to meet some people."

"Do I need to bring a book or a snack?" Hanna asked. Yes, it would be great to get out of her tiny apartment and mingle with people who weren't looking for faucets and electrical wiring.

"If you want to, that's fine, but don't worry about it, if you don't. We always have too much. Give me your phone number and I will text you the address and time."

"Sounds wonderful," Hannah said. "Really appreciate you inviting me."

"Hey, it's great to have some fresh blood in town," Jess said. "Come on, Sam, we have some more errands to run."

"Bye, Sam, bye, Jess, see you tonight," Hannah said, as she turned back to her shelf stocking. Something fun to do tonight, rather than go home and surf the web.

"Hey, Hannah, I'm taking off," Hunter said. "Kevin's coming in at three to close, but you knew that." Kevin was their new hire and it would be his first night closing alone. She'd plan to pop back in right before closing and just make sure he was okay.

"Yeah, I knew that. Doing anything this afternoon?"

"Going fishing," he said. "Gotta get the good out of my new boat." Macintyre had a gorgeous lake that it skirted, called Lake Constance, that he'd parked his boat on and fished there as often as he could. She always thought it was because of the lake that he'd agreed to move down here with her. She didn't care why;

she was just glad he had. Affording this place alone would have been impossible.

"Have fun, I'll see you tomorrow." She waved at him. They rarely hung out together, even though they got along great, but working together at the store and being business partners was enough closeness, they both thought. However, they both knew the other had their back, no matter what. Sometimes she thought he was bossy and annoying. Sometimes she knew he thought she was just a royal pain, but none of that mattered in the long term. They were family and business partners and quasi friends.

"You ready for a break?" she asked Tonya a few hours later. "Go take your twenty." She opened the other register. There had been a couple rushes earlier, but it was slow right now. She looked around, Tonya had gotten most of the candy restocked under the registers between customers, which was a good thing. They were a nice little spur of the moment grab for most people who came through and certainly for the kids they brought with them. Every dollar helped.

"Good..." she glanced at the clock, "Good afternoon, Mr. Berry." He was one of their regulars who often came in to just look around. He'd retired a few years ago and said his job now was puttering around his house, so he was often in to pick up something or just get ideas. Hannah thought he often came in just to chatter. There were a couple areas in the store that she felt were underutilized. Maybe she'd put a coffee pot and a few rocking chairs in one of them, like an old-fashioned general store where people could come and just visit. The more people in the store meant the more things they would buy. In the other corner, she wanted to do a little gift shop, with items that were homemade by people in Macintyre. That would bring more women into the shop, also a good thing. The holidays were coming and she wanted a large slice of the holiday shopping dollars pie. Hannah shivered in utter happiness and anticipation. When

Tonya came back from her break, she headed to the back room to work on orders and paperwork.

Sitting down at her small desk, she shivered again. Derrick. Hawk. Whatever his name was. What was it about that man? She had never had such a visceral reaction to any person before. Not even kittens made her that crazy, and she loved kittens. As soon as she bought a house, she'd be getting another cat. Her cat, George, was ten years old, but she got him as a five-year-old rescue. She really wanted a kitten, just for the excitement of having something lively in the house. Who didn't love a kitten? What if Derrick Hawk was allergic to cats?

Giggling, Hannah opened the computer program and got to work. What was she thinking? Who knew? It was ridiculous. The entire thing. He was divorced with a nineteen-year-old son. She did know that now, after a little questioning of Tonya who knew a lot, almost as much as Rodney did. She was less than ten years older than his kid, so that made him less than the twenty years older than her that she'd guessed. It had been the silver streaks in his hair, she imagined. Probably genetic, but she liked it. He might be seeing someone for all she knew. Why would he be interested in someone like her? He probably had to beat them off with sticks. She'd let him beat her with a stick if he wanted. If she ever saw him again, and she reacted like she did today, yeah. Whatever.

Laughing at herself, she got back to work and put her stupid nonsense behind her. She had a girls' night to go to later and she felt excited about it, but knew she'd have to leave early to come check on Kevin on her way home.

"Hey, Jer, don't forget to grab your books on your way out. See you Saturday, thank you for all your hard work today."

"It's kinda what you pay me to do," he smiled at her and waved on his way out to his afternoon classes. "See you Saturday."

He was a good kid. His dad had raised him well. Rolling her

eyes, she thought, well, that was about a minute and a half she hadn't thought about Derrick or Hawk, she'd have to see which he preferred. Good job, Han, she told herself. Keep it up!

A few hours later, she'd been interrupted six times with questions and customers, but finished the payroll and the schedule for the next two weeks, and sent in the supply order for the month. Plus she ordered a huge coffee pot and a stand kit for it to go on. She'd started looking for a few chairs to go around it, too. She'd have her cozy little coffee corner before winter, a little gathering spot for the men to sit around in the mornings, or women to meet with their knitting or whatever. Maybe she could hold a few classes later on down the road on how to do simple repairs and things she'd grown up knowing and had been very surprised when she got to college that many didn't. Different lifestyles. That would fit well into her cozy corner, too. Glancing at the clock, she went to make sure that the store wasn't crazy busy and that everything was in order before she went home. Kevin would be here in less than an hour to take over for the night. She'd go home, shower and change, grab something to eat and head over to Jessie's house. It was nice to have evening plans that didn't involve laundry and TV for a change.

"Come on in, Hannah," Jess said, opening the pretty blue door to her adorable little stone house.

"Thanks, I love your house!" she said.

"Want to buy it?" Jess asked, leading the way into a cozy little living room that featured a huge rock fireplace. She had never seen anything as eye catching, she loved it! She could picture a Christmas tree there in the corner, a cheerful fire, and cookies and hot chocolate, waiting to be consumed.

"What?" Hannah looked at her. Had she heard right?

"We're putting it on the market next month. Mac and I are

building a house on the edge of town, as you know, because I've been in so often to pick stuff out for that one and to get this one ready to go on the market. I ask everyone if they want to buy it."

"I am actually in the market for a house," Hannah said. "I'm living in a tiny apartment and it's a little crowded between me and George."

"George?" Jess asked as they walked into the kitchen.

"My cat," she laughed, looking at the small but adorable kitchen where three other women sat.

"Oh, I thought I was hearing some news," Jess said. "This is Emmy, you need to know her, she's a fantastic realtor. Hannah is looking for a house, if she doesn't fall in love with mine."

"Oh, great to meet you," Emmy said, moving her dark hair away from her face. "You working with anyone yet?"

Hannah shook her head. "I haven't officially started looking yet. I've been waiting until my schedule settles down some and it's starting to, so, soon!"

"Hannah and her brother Hunter own the Double H hardware store downtown," Jess said. "They just moved here. This is Bronwyn."

"You I've seen in the store," Hannah said, shaking her hand.

"Yeah, I took over my dad's plumbing business and pop in for things now and then," Bronwyn said.

"Oh, that's right, we've talked a few times." Hannah remembered now. She'd met so many new people.

"This is Marnie, she's Sam's babysitter," Jess said, "and I think Tori will be here later on."

Marnie shook her head, "I don't think she's going to make it tonight. She's has conferences tonight."

"Oh, that's right," Jess said. "I knew that. She told me when I picked up Sam today. Tori runs the day care I take Sam to," she explained to Hannah. "Pregnancy brain."

"Oh, congratulations," she said. "I didn't know."

"I'm not showing yet," Jess said as if that explained everything. "Have a seat, I'll pour the wine I can't have. Then I'll show you around the house, if you want to see it."

"I'd love to see it," Hannah said as she settled on one of the bar stools at the butcher block island. She didn't really cook, but she liked a nice kitchen.

"Help yourself," Emmy motioned toward the platter of cookies and other delicacies on the counter. "We are all frustrated bakers and Jess and Marnie are the only ones with a man to feed, so we tend to bring stuff all the time."

"Do you do this often?" Hannah asked, picking up an oatmeal cookie. "Thank you."

"We try to every couple of weeks, sometimes more often and sometimes less when life gets busy," Marnie said.

"I think that is great," Hannah said. "I hope I fit in." She took a drink of the wine that Jess handed her and smiled. "Now, that is good wine."

"I think you will fit in just fine," Emmy said, and clinked glasses with her. Hannah noted that Emmy had lemonade in hers. Was she pregnant, too? Or maybe she was the designated driver?

Hannah sat and mostly listened, only interjecting enough to be friendly as she got to know her new friends. She learned Jess was hoping for twins, apparently Mac had a twin sister who died and had been Jessie's best friend. Marnie had gotten married right out of college and used to teach, but was now a stay at home mom to a toddler and a three-month-old, while going back to school online and watching Sam a couple days a week but hoped to start teaching again this fall. Bronwyn was single and seemed to enjoy her job as a plumber, a lot. Like she and Hunter had, Bronwyn grew up in her dad's business and took it over when he retired. He was in fact, the Mr. Berry who came into the shop and hung around sometimes. Emmy, too, was single and working her way up in the real estate business. She wasn't certain that was going to be her forever career, but she enjoyed it for now, and the freedom it gave her to go horseback riding as often as she could. She competed in rodeos which Hannah didn't understand. Wasn't that bucking bulls and things? She'd never been to a rodeo. Maybe a new experience at some point for her?

"Come and see the house," Jess told her a little later on. "I'd love not have to go through the hassle of putting it up for sale, if you are really serious about wanting a house, but if you don't want it, that is no problem. Don't worry about it."

"I heard that," Emmy laughed. "I'll come, too. I know the house, but will do the walk through in case I end up listing it."

"Oh, the pressure," Hannah said, laughing as she got up. "So far it is adorable." They walked through the three-bedroom house, saw a partial basement and an oddly large backyard and patio, all set up for grilling.

"In the new house, there's a place for a swing set and enough room we can put in a garden and maybe a swimming pool when the kids get older," Jess said. "I hate leaving my garden, but it will be fun to plan something new. I have peonies over there, a little strawberry bed, and you can see where the rest of my garden is. There are tulips and daffodils in the spring, too. I love growing tomatoes and have a small herb garden in the side yard."

Hannah could feel herself falling in love with it, despite all the garden things she doubted she'd ever use. She didn't cook. But falling in love? That was twice in one day, she must have some weird hormone thing going on. First Hawk and now this house. What? She wasn't in love with Derrick Hawk, she was just... attracted to him, admired him as an older man. Something. Shaking her head, she listened to Jess talk about her new house they were building.

"The only downside to this house is that it only has one bathroom," Jess said. "When I lived here by myself, it wasn't a big deal, but since Mac and Sam moved in, it's presented some challenges." She opened a door that led to a small room that held a washer and dryer, the hot water heater and furnace. "Mac was going to build a small powder room in here, but then he got busy with his new job and the other house and it didn't happen."

"That would really enhance the value of the house," Emmy pointed out.

"We know," Jess agreed. "But I don't think it will be a big enough deal that the next person wouldn't be able to see the vision. Plus, I've talked to both Bronwyn and Hawk and we would roll the cost of it into the sale price if that was a deal breaker for someone."

"I want it," Hannah said, shocking herself.

"The powder room?" Emmy asked while Jessie looked at her as if she were nuts.

"No, I want to buy the house." Why were these words coming out of her mouth? She hadn't looked at the housing market yet, or neighborhoods or anything, but something about this house just hit her. She didn't even know how much it was! It just felt right, felt like home already. It was only about fifteen minutes to work, there was a small sunroom off the kitchen with a little table and chairs in it now, but she'd probably put a love seat in there for George. It would be a lovely place to sit and have coffee before work. She'd hire someone to look after the yard and maybe she'd learn to cook? Who knew?

"Am I good or what?" Emmy asked Jessie. Then she looked at Hannah and said, "Your next day off, call me and we will go to the office and go over numbers and things, okay?"

Three months later, Hannah sat in the middle of her boxes, looking around her new living room. Her brother and some of his friends would be here with her bed, couch and a few other things she'd brought from Missouri when they moved. Jessie and Mac had moved out the weekend before, and had started the new powder room for her as a sort of surprise housewarming gift. Emmy assured her the cost had been rolled into the price of the house, so they weren't really paying for the entire thing, but still, it was very sweet of them to get it set up and the work started. She adored Jessie and while Mac intimidated her a little at first, she found him to be a very loving dad and husband.

Walking around the house, she walked into what used to be Sam's bedroom and pondered the pink wall. It was very odd for a toddler boy's room, but why not? She actually liked the color, though the other walls being red, she wasn't so sure about. How hard would it be to cover up the red? Jessie had offered to paint it, but she told her no. She didn't want the pregnant woman painting and she didn't yet know her theme or what she wanted the color of this room to be. For now, it didn't really matter. But, pink for a boy? How sexist was she that she thought it was strange?

The third bedroom, painted a very light sunshine yellow, was smaller and she thought she'd use it for her home office. She had a tech coming out in a few days to set up the computer to access the one at work so she could do payroll, ordering, bill paying and schedules on either at any time, without swapping flash drives back and forth. Her new bedroom was a lovely shade of periwinkle blue which matched or coordinated with none of her bedding and curtains, which were all autumn shades. But she had time to decide to either paint the room or buy new stuff, that was part of the fun of a new house.

The living room was what Jessie had called jailhouse gray, and said Mac demanded it when they were thinking of putting the house on the market, but she didn't mind it. Jessie seemed to hate it which amused her. The floors were all a lighter hard wood throughout the entire house, but for the bathroom and laundry room, which were both a white tile, and she felt at home for the first time since her parents had sold their house and moved to Florida to be close to her mom's sister while she battled her cancer.

Hearing her doorbell, she frowned. Okay, that sound had to change. She could probably change the doorbell out. She wasn't quite as handy as people often thought she was. She knew a bit about a lot of things, mostly from osmosis and hanging around the store and helping out. She knew she wasn't as handy as Bronwyn or as crafty and cute as Jessie, but… She needed to do it.

"Derrick Hawk!"

At her door. Standing in front of her. Breathing.

Chapter 2

Okay, she sounded way too happy to see him. She needed to tone that down. "I'm surprised to see you," she said. See how normal she sounded? Yeah. Normal was a good thing.

She'd seen him in the store a few times and tried to stay away from him because he made her heart hammer and her brain go fuzzy. Her fingers shook and her entire body had a reaction to him. She checked him out once and accidently gave him twenty dollars too much in change and would never have known if he hadn't told her. What did he do to her? Could he stop? Why was he here?

He had a toolbox in his hand and looked at her quizzically, "I'm here to work on your new bathroom," he said. "Did you not know?"

"For some reason, I thought it was Bronwyn doing it," she confessed and stepped back. "I'm moving in today." Like he needed to know that. Well, he probably did need to know that. There would be guys swarming the place soon, carrying in her furniture.

"Umm, come in." OMG Derrick Hawk was in her house. In

her house. Mouth dry, she walked toward the room where he would be working. Had she brushed her hair today? What was she wearing? Her stupid ripped jeans and an old baggy tee shirt. Yeah, way to make an impression. Did she care? Nope, she did not. Not one bit. Maybe a little bit. Could she go change? No makeup either. She just thought it was going to be all sweat and dirt today. And Hunter with his friends who didn't matter to her, and now Derrick – Hawk—What should she call him?—was in her house.

Deep breath, girl, get over yourself. Opening the door to the laundry, soon-to-be-powder, room, she said, "This was rolled into the sale of the house, I don't quite know what Jessie and Mac wanted done."

He smiled at her, and she had to grab the edge of the door jamb to steady herself. The man made her knees weak. Asinine. She had this. "Well, I have the budget so let's see what you are thinking and I will see what we can do within that budget. Don't worry, we will figure it out. I've done this before."

Hannah bit her tongue not to say, "Whatever you need, I'll come up with it!" She'd just bought a house and a business! She was maxed out right now, she couldn't be spending anymore, no matter how much time him putting in a spa would take and he would be in her house doing it. No. Just no.

"I hadn't thought too much about it," she confessed. "I know a toilet and sink for sure, and I wouldn't mind a little shower in here if that fit in the budget and the space. If not, I can do without it."

"Hannah, we're here!" she heard Hunter call from the front door.

"You go ahead," Derrick said. "I'll work up some plans and we can talk again in a bit."

Yes! She was going to talk to him in a bit! That made her heart pitter patter and she knew she had the goofiest grin on her face as she went to help Hunter unload the truck. He'd brought his buddy Ryan and Jessie's husband Mac to help. Between the four of them, it shouldn't take long to unload her bedroom and living room furniture, which was all she had. She'd already moved most of the boxes filled with clothes, kitchen things, pictures and books. Other things she'd ordered online which would magically show up at her door at some point next week and still others she'd be getting in the future. No hurry. She planned to be here in this cozy little house for a long time and was in no rush to get everything done. She'd just enjoy the process of being settled in her sweet little house for a long time.

"I'm ready! Let's get this done!"

Hunter pushed back his starting to get shaggy blond hair, and said, "Just tell us where you want it."

"Bull hockey," she said. "I'm not a weakling, I can carry."

"No one said you were a weakling," Mac told her. "But it hurts the male ego to see little girls carry things."

Hannah giggled at him. "Poor male egos. Such fragile things." She watched Mac as he picked up the edge of a love seat and she grabbed the other end. She'd overheard him talking to Jessie one day when she'd been over measuring for curtains. They had been in the kitchen and she'd heard Jessie let out a sob and felt horrible. It had to be hard to leave this house. Hannah knew it was their choice to sell it and build a new home, but she understood the regret. Then she'd heard Mac ask Jessie something so odd, he'd said, *"Do you need a good paddling, baby?"* in a voice that didn't sound threatening at all but filled with love and concern. Then Jessie had said, *"Probably."* Weird, weird, weird. What was that all about? She didn't understand it, but hey, they seemed happy together, so whatever floated your boat or frosted your cookies or whatever. She'd finished measuring for the curtains, and Jessie had come out with a glass of tea and they'd chatted about the house as if things were just fine. It was nothing she would ever ask about.

She thought about it though, every time she saw Mac. It

niggled at her brain, and made her think things she'd put to the side for a long time. She'd hadn't even had a date in over a year now, since they first started talking about the store. The girls' nights she'd had a couple times with Jessie, Marnie, Emmy, Bronwyn, and Tori were as close as she got to a social life. That was fine for now, between her work, remodeling the store for her little nooks, building the business, moving and now also remodeling a bathroom, that she hoped would take a really long time, she had her hands, and life full. Hawk would be in her house almost every day for a long time. How long? Maybe he would tell her when he finished the plans? What if she couldn't manage to behave herself, and acted like a silly fangirl every time she saw him? What would he do? She didn't know, but she wanted to know and, what the man did to her brain was just wrong in so many ways.

"Hannah, I don't mind standing here waiting for you to decide, but your arms are shaking," Mac said as she noticed they were standing in the living room. She didn't even remember carrying it in there.

"In front of the fireplace for now," she said, trying desperately not to blush. He couldn't read her mind. He just thought she was standing there trying to decide where to put the love seat.

Right. The way he grinned at her made her blush harder, so she put her end down and fled toward the kitchen where, unfortunately, Hawk—had she decided to call him Hawk?—sat at the island. His laptop in front of him, and she wanted nothing more than to be his laptop. Or on his lap. Something.

"Couple of options for you," he said, "if you have a minute."

His voice. Dang his voice. It made her want to purr. Just crawl up on his lap and put her arms around his neck and purr. She'd never met a guy who made her feel like that before.

"Why don't you get a drink?" Derrick suggested. "You look pretty warm."

Well, she was, but not in the way he thought. Walking to the refrigerator, she pulled out a couple cans of soda and put one in front of him and took another for herself. Popping open the top, she took a big drink. It wasn't as refreshing as they claimed on TV. She had an idea what might be, but focused on looking at the picture on his laptop, instead of thinking of that.

"Now, that is a fancy program," she said. It was 3D and everything, just like the ones on TV she saw sometimes while channel surfing.

"Okay, here is the first one," he said. "It's just adding in the toilet here and vanity with a sink there. Not moving the washer or dryer."

"Okay, looks a little cramped," she said. "But adequate."

"Here's two more," he said, "all in the budget I was given."

She couldn't figure out how the last one with the tiled shower stall, moving the washer and dryer to the other wall, putting in a toilet enclosed on the back wall and a big soaker sink instead of a vanity was the same price as just the toilet and sink. She worked in a hardware store, she knew the prices of things, but she also knew the last one would take longer. Which, of course, meant having Hawk hanging around her house more. She needed to lose ten pounds and get her hair cut. Where did that come from?

"And it's all in the budget?" she asked him, dubiously.

"Some of it is way under and yes, they are all in budget," he assured her. "What do you think?"

"Number three," she said as if that was the one she wanted and not the one that would keep him working in her house longer. She just wanted to be with, no, just near him. What was wrong with her?

"Han, where do you want this?" Hunter shouted from the other room.

"Go," Hawk said. "We can go over finishes and things a little later." He looked at his watch. He still wore a watch. How old was he? "I have almost an hour before I have to be at my next appointment. I'll come help unload the truck."

"Oh, you don't have to do that," she said.

"But I want to," he said.

What was she going to say to that? "Thank you." Thank you was a good cover all. Like she was going to tell him not to help. Heck, no, the man needed to hang around as much as possible! Just because. No other reason needed.

She directed Hunter to the living room and then followed Hawk out to the truck. He picked up her dresser and she grabbed a couple drawers and followed him down the ramp. The man was strong. Of course he was. Why wouldn't he be? He worked with his hands for a living.

"Bedroom, I assume?" he said as they walked in the house.

There went her mouth again, all drying out and her heart pattering. Yes, please, sir. Luckily, she managed not to say it through her dry mouth. "Second door," she managed though. See how well she was doing? Like she was a real grown adult and everything.

The truck was unloaded within the hour and all the guys disappeared. She planned on feeding them, but Hunter said they were all going to his boat for the afternoon. Hawk left at the same time they did to go to another job, and she was happy to be alone in her own house. Yes, why yes, she was. Taking the paper he had sketched out to leave with her, she walked into the small laundry room and looked around. Even though she lived here alone, it would be wonderful to have a second bathroom. One day she could need or want a roommate or meet someone, or just even if she had a party or two. Had a kid. Two bathrooms were a good thing. Man, Derrick Hawk was hot. What else could she need done when he finished this? Did he paint? What was his title? Contractor, plumber, electrician, what?

Finishes. She needed to think of finishes. Did she want a common theme throughout the house? Yeah, she did. She wanted a Hawk themed house. He could be her common theme. Right now, she had to start unpacking boxes and make her bed.

Her first night in her new house, and she opened in the morning, so had to be to bed early. Someone had to work and make her house payment and it might as well be her.

A few days later, she opened her door to Hawk again. "How are you, pretty lady?" He smiled at her and she did not swoon. Nope. She didn't. As an adult, she just smiled back at him.

"Hi! I have the room cleaned out and ready for you."

He walked in, carrying his laptop and a tool belt. "I'm ready to get started this morning. You are going to be sick of seeing me before this is over."

Somehow, she doubted that seriously. "Two things. Here is where I keep the grocery list. If you want a certain kind of drink or snack or anything, you can add it on here, or if you want to bring your own and use the fridge or microwave or whatever, help yourself, whether I'm here or not."

He had no idea what he did to her, how he affected her. His presence just attacked her entire physical being. There was not one part of her that didn't feel him. Weird. She even felt weird around his kid at work now, and tended to avoid him rather than interact with him. What was wrong? Pheromones? Hormones? She probably just needed to take the man to bed and get it over with. Bursting into giggles, she covered her mouth to stifle them as he followed her to the soon to be bathroom.

"What is number two?" he asked her.

Number two? Oh yeah. Do it, girl, she told herself. "What do I call you? Derrick, Hawk, Mr. Hawk? What?"

"Hawk is fine. Derrick is okay too. I answer to about anything."

"Except Dad," she said. She should not have said that.

"Yeah, the kid hung out at work with me all the time until he started school. Everyone else called me Hawk, so he did, too. I never minded."

So that was that. Hawk it was. For now.

"I'm working from home this morning," she told him. "Doing supply orders and schedules, so if you need anything, just come get me, okay? I'll be in the office."

"Will do," Derrick watched her walk away and sighed. What was he thinking? She was his kid's age. Or close to it, she was older than Jer by a few years but still closer to Jer's age than his. He wasn't a man who went chasing after young things. His wife had left when Jer was three and while she was in and out of his life, he'd been a twenty-three-year-old man raising a son alone for the most part. Since then, he'd gone to trade school and built his business. Macintyre was a good place to raise a child and Jer was turning out to be a good man. He worked hard at the hardware store, and was going to the local college, getting ready to go to state college in January. His own life was stable, solid and sorely lacking in the love department, except for casual dates. He never seemed to lack those, but never seemed interested in having more than a couple with any one woman.

When he met Hannah, first saw her at her hardware store, he'd fallen in... what, lust? Surely not love for the pretty little blonde who knew her way around tools, hardware, business and seemed to have her life together. He had underbid this job purposefully to get it when he found out what it was and who it was for. He wanted to be in her house, near her and just see what had happened to make him want to have her. Have her? Yeah. In more ways than one. He might think she was an adorable little thing, but he had rules about his life and the people in it, which was, he admitted, probably why he had never been able to keep a woman. Would he change for this woman? Probably not. Would she adapt to him? Probably not. Or who knew what life would bring? Maybe they would be a perfect fit. He snorted as he looked at his plans for her new bathroom, again. Yeah, that pretty, intelligent, blonde thing would want him around. She probably looked at him as a father figure. He didn't mind that. He could be Daddy. Daddy with benefits? Was that weird? Did he care? Not really. For now, though, he would be friendly, work on her bathroom and just see where things went and what happened.

He looked around, noting the room had been well cleaned out. That was good. Going into places and having to clean it out before he started a job cost both the homeowner money because he charged for it, and him time he didn't want to spend. He was careful with both his time and money. He worked on a set schedule and regimented both his exercise time and his eating habits. His son called him anal retentive and didn't realize he considered that a compliment. He liked his regulated life he could control, and while he had come to realize he couldn't, didn't need to control, Jer any longer, it was still tempting to step in. Jer didn't need him to do that, however. Jer had his own life and at age forty-two, Derrick realized it was time for him to have one, too.

Hitting the gym every morning at five didn't really count as a social life. Soon Jer would be off to state college and he'd be going to an empty home all the time, instead of just once in a while when Jer was out. He'd be an empty nester and would have decades of life ahead of him to do what, work? And then retire, to what? Feeling at odds with his emotions and his own life? That was not in his plans. His focus for the last almost twenty years had been to provide for, and raise his son to be a good man. He'd done both and now what? Was that why he was letting a bit of a blonde distract him? She didn't need him to raise her, she seemed to be doing just fine. She also didn't look like the one-night-stand kind and a woman her age would probably want to start a family. Did he want to have kids now at his age? His brain seemed to be working triple time on stupid things, so Derrick grabbed his hammer, went over to the wall that was coming down and started to work. Getting worn out was the best solution.

Hannah jumped hearing the noise, then smiled. He got right to work, didn't he? She headed to her office to do the supply orders and schedules. One of her pet peeves when she'd worked retail during college were stores that didn't schedule you out longer than a week. It had been frustrating to not know what days you had off or had to work and caused a lot more drama than needed when people made plans and then found out a day or two before they had to work instead. She could run a store with as little drama as possible and with a great work environment, at least that was her plan. Happy employees made for happy customers. Schedules out a couple weeks were an important part of that.

After working a couple hours, she took a break and checked her email. Hannah flipped to that screen and frowned after reading one from her friend Sherri. That wasn't good at all. She walked into the kitchen, poured a couple glasses of lemonade and walked over to the soon to be powder room. Wow, he was just getting it done.

"You don't look happy," he said, reaching for the icy glass she offered him. "Something wrong?"

"Oh, I just got some bad news from a friend," she said.

"Your friend okay?" he asked.

"No, she actually just got arrested with her boyfriend for selling drugs," she admitted. "I'm kind of in shock."

"Cut her off," he said, looking at her with those piercing gray eyes. "You don't need to be associating with people like that."

"She's my friend! Hannah looked at him, surprised. "You don't just cut people off because they made a mistake."

"Selling drugs isn't a mistake, it's a choice," he said.

Well, he had something there. "I understand what you are saying," she said. "But cutting off a friend who needs at least moral support right now, is not who I am."

"How can you give her moral support? What are you going to do, say 'good job, get away with it better next time' or what?"

"Wow, have you never made a mistake in your life? If you messed up my bathroom, I wouldn't cut you off."

Derrick laughed and she felt a flash of irritation, even while she had to admit that was a stupid analogy. "Okay, if Jer walked out of the store with something in his pocket he'd forgotten he put in there…" No, that still wouldn't work. Accidents were not the same thing as drug dealing.

She sighed. "I don't know. It's just, I mean, how do you wrap your head around something like that? It just isn't something you think of someone you know doing. Sure, partying in college is one thing, but this? I don't know. It's just…"

"Bad, illegal, wrong, stupid, immoral, dangerous," he supplied.

Hannah rolled her eyes at him and sipped her lemonade, then said, "Yeah, I guess."

"The line between right and wrong is specific," he said.

"There are many shades of gray," she reminded him.

"Don't tell me you read that book." He smiled at her and her body reminded her just how flat out attractive the man was.

"Couple of times," she said, and raised her eyebrows at him. "You?"

"Listened to it in my truck."

She choked on her drink. "You did not!"

"Are you calling me a liar, young lady?"

"I might be," she giggled, feeling a little better for some reason. He came off all stern and rigid, but seemed to have a playful side.

"Little girls who call names might find their fannies warmed properly," he said.

"Fannies?" Okay, that made her smile harder and feel, well, she wasn't sure how she felt. Turned on? Interested? She'd already been interested, but he probably thought of her like a peer to his son, not someone he might be interested in. In what? Dating? Making love to? Paddling her fanny? Who said fanny? He did. Sounded like something her grandpa would say. Did he mean it? She could imagine being across his knee, and having her 'fanny' warmed then being held and cuddled after. What? Where was her brain? Her brain needed to go back to work.

Oh and she, no, someone vaguely called 'rolled into the price' was paying him by the hour. Or the job or something. She didn't actually know, which didn't say a lot for her actual business skill, which she had a lot of. Truth was, she'd been so excited about the fact he was coming, she didn't check into it. She vowed to do that. It made business sense to know it and why was her brain running in circles again? She had no idea. The man just did something to her and why was he looking at her like that? Shaking her head, she noticed her hand trembled as she reached for his glass. No, it didn't. Yeah, it did and when his fingers brushed against hers, so did her knees. Heart hammering, she turned to go put the glasses up, and he said, "Thanks for the drink and that is a nice fanny."

Shaking her head, she went back to the kitchen. He was teasing her, that was all. Like older guys often did. They should be more PC, but really, she'd grown up in a hardware store around plumbers, farmers, truckers, mechanics, anyone who fixed anything and most of them had a, what she called, broad sense of humor. She learned to let it roll off her, most of them meant nothing by it, most of them were trying to be friendly. As long as they kept their hands to themselves, and there had been less than a handful who hadn't over the years, she'd been fine. She could deal and either shut them down or play with them a little and leave them laughing. Never taking them seriously was the key. So why did she feel as if she needed to take Derrick seriously? While she wasn't Spock, she knew it wasn't logical. None of it was, but she had work to do.

Shooting off a short email to Sherri, she commiserated, and

told her to let her know if there was anything she could do. Why she felt guilty about offering, she didn't know. Sure she did. Hawk. He was the one who made her feel that way.

Then she turned back on her work screen and buckled down. She wanted to get this done. Tomorrow was truck day and she had to be at work at 4 a.m. and wouldn't get off until 4 p.m. when Kevin came in to take over the evening shift. She wanted to get done with the paperwork so she could go out shopping this afternoon. Tomorrow at work, she'd make another key to hide outside, so she could give one to Hawk so he could come and go as he wanted. In fact, she suddenly decided, she was giving him one today. What were the odds she would lose her keys or lock herself out of the house tonight?

Going back to the kitchen, she slid her key off her key ring and reminded herself to replace it with the one that was in the bowl on her dresser. She'd been meaning to hide it outside, but hadn't done it yet. Too much else to do. That was a good thing because now she had a spare for her key ring.

Waiting until he was done for the day, she walked in as he was packing up and looked around. "Wow, you've done a lot today."

"I work hard," he said, simply, putting tools back in his carrier. "I'll try to get it done on deadline."

"No hurry," she said for some weird reason she didn't understand. "Here's a key to my house. You can come and go as you want but I'd sure appreciate a text or a call letting me know when you'll be coming, just so I'm not surprised." Okay, now that she was in front of him again, she wanted her key back. Wanting to be here when he was here was just... normal, right? Of course it was. Most people were home when the worker people were there. But he already put it on his keyring so it was sort of too late to ask for it back and there went her stupid brain racing around about stupid things in front of him. How did he do what he did to her and have no clue? It just was not right.

"I have your number, do you have mine saved in your phone?" he asked. "Let me see."

Let him see? Let him see her phone. Why not? She punched in her password and handed it over. See what a good little girl, who did not need her fanny warmed, she was? He looked at her phone, then added a number. "The first is my work number, the second is my personal number. Just in case I accidently text or call you from that one." Sure. She just bet he accidently did that a lot. Not. From what Jer said about him, he was quite precise. Which wasn't quite the term Jer used but precise was appropriate.

"Thank you," she said, because she wasn't going to quiz him on how often he texted people from the 'wrong' number. That would just be, well, 'wrong'.

"I'm heading out," he said, then paused and asked, "you have any plans for tonight?"

She shook her head, heart hammering and mouth dry.

"Let me go home and clean up and change and we can grab a bite to eat if you want? I think both of us skipped lunch today."

He was right, so she forced her head to move the other way, into a nod. Yes, please, she wanted to go eat with him. "I have a truck in the morning, but I could grab something quick with you." Her mouth worked again! Yay!

"Be back in about an hour," he said and left. She watched him walk down the sidewalk to his truck and sighed. The man was fine. More than fine. He'd asked her out. Right? Why? He was hungry and wanted company? Of course. What other reason could there be. What should she wear? What did one wear for a casual bite to eat? No way could even the amazing Amazon bring her some new clothes in the next hour. Surely she had something in her closet. Of course, she did. What was wrong with her and why did her heart feel as if it were beating out of her chest? She was being ridiculous. Probably just needed her fanny warmed. Giggling, she pulled out a casual tee shirt dress, put on some makeup and a pair of dangling earrings she could never wear to work.

There. She was all ready for a casual bite to eat with the guy renovating her bathroom. Why that made her giggle, too, well… nerves. It was nerves. That was all. She was attracted to the man. Probably being in close contact with him, and the frustrations that came with any reno would change that. She had nothing to worry about and her poor fanny had the very least to worry about. Which was a bit of a shame, but there you go.

She stood by the door and waited for her date, no, for her casual bite to eat, no, for the man taking her for the casual bite to eat. One day her brain would work again, she felt certain. Until then, she decided, she would simply enjoy the feeling of being a giddy kid in love. What? No, a giddy kid in lust? In having a crush? Something, but she was going along for the ride.

The ride? Hawk pulled up in something that was not his work truck. It was a low-slung fancy, cherry red sports car thing. She didn't know cars well, but she knew this one had to be an old and expensive classic convertible. Reaching into the hall closet, she grabbed the first ball cap she saw, to keep her hair out of her eyes, and from flying all over, slapped her pocket to check for her phone, where she kept some cash and a rarely used credit card tucked away in the case, and ran out the door, locking it behind her, to admire him. The car. To admire the car, of course, though the man looked just fine as he got out of the car and walked around to open the door for her.

"I was expecting your truck," she said. "This is gorgeous." And again, she meant the car.

"I live out of that truck twelve hours a day," he said. "My off time, I like to have a little fun. Restored her myself," he said proudly.

"In your off time?" she said. "You work as much as I do."

"Hard to build a business," he said, holding her elbow as she got into the car. "You and I both know that. I was a single dad when I started, working for my uncle. He sold the business to me about ten years later."

"What happened to Jer's mom, if you don't mind me asking?" she asked watching him get into his side of the car.

"She took off for city lights when Jer was three," he said, starting the car which turned over and purred. Nice.

"Does she come back?" Hannah asked, curious.

"Off and on. She pops in and out of Jer's life. It used to bug him when he was small, but as he grew up, he came to realize it was just her way."

Hannah imagined it still bugged him, but she decided not to say anything. She put her hat on and settled back to enjoy the ride. "If I owned this, I'd be living out of it, instead of the truck," she told him.

"Yeah, like I would throw tools and put my muddy boots in her. She wouldn't like that one bit," Derrick said.

"It's a car," Hannah teased him. "It doesn't have feelings!"

Derrick shot her a look that made her giggle. "Watch your mouth, little girl! If she gets her feelings hurt, you are walking home!"

"In these shoes?"

She stretched her feet out to show off her obviously only semi-practical sandals.

"Nah, I wouldn't make you walk far in those, " he said. "That would be just wrong."

"I know," she agreed. "And I imagine you are the kind of guy who doesn't like to be wrong."

Shooting her a look, he asked, "What makes you think that?"

What did make her think that? Just watch your words, she thought. "Just that you have an air of confidence, and authority." Were those the right words?

"I appreciate that," he said, and rubbed the scruff on the side of his face, then he obviously changed the subject. "So how do you like Macintyre? Seem to be settling in okay? Getting to know people?" He pulled up in front of a small Mexican restaurant that boasted the best shrimp and chorizo mixed grill in the state. The place looked a little too cookie cutter to her to be a best in the state, but maybe it was, she would be happy to just have something someone else cooked, because her cooking mostly sucked.

"I love it. I have a few new friends, and I love my store. I loved working for my dad, but having my own and being able to make my own decisions is even better."

"Nothing like owning your own business," he agreed. "Being in charge is the best, isn't it? I can't imagine working for someone else. Of course, you have your brother to run things by."

She laughed, just a little, "Well, we both work by the rule, 'it's often better to beg forgiveness than ask permission' and while that seems weird, we are both on the same track so often, it really works for us. I'm not constantly bombarding him with things and vice versa. We have a once a week meeting to go over things and other than that, we both just run the store. I have a blast working in the store, but he does it just to have the money for his boat. Work and go boating, it's all he cares about."

"His boat?" Hawk asked.

"Or boats. I think he has two now, and this time next year, he will have a few more. If he could find a way to live on the water, he would."

Hawk got out and she smiled as he walked around to the car door to open it for her, then held out his hand to help her out of the low-slung car. That was nice. She never had a guy open a car door for her before. Well, once when her girl scout troop took a limo to the ballet when she was a kid. That had been a reward for selling cookies, and it had been a magical night, as she recalled, including the handsome limo driver who poured them all sparkling juice in fancy glasses to drink on the way there.

Walking into the small, dark diner with Hawk at her side, seemed just as magical. Even though this looked like a normal, family friendly little diner/cafe, with him, it seemed amazing, sparkling and she saw everything through a filtered lens of... what? Lust? Probably. She didn't know the man well enough to feel anything else.

"Hello, Hawk," the hostess said. "Two tonight?"

"Evening, Remmie," he said to the woman who appeared to be a little older than he was, and Hannah looked her over. Hmm. "This is Hannah, she's new in town, she and her brother own the Double H hardware store downtown."

"Welcome to Macintyre," Remmie said, leading them to a small booth. "You will love it, and I hope you come back here often, and bring all the friends a pretty girl like you is bound to make."

Hannah smiled, but felt irritated for some reason. "Thank you," she said politely. Remmie handed them both menus and put the wrapped silverware on the table.

"See you, Hawk," she said. And she said it in a way that Hannah knew what it meant.

"So you and Remmie?" she asked when she was out of earshot and back at the hostess station, chatting to a family that walked in.

"Me and Remmie?" he looked at her, and seemed surprised.

"Yeah."

"No," he said. "Well…"

"So, yes?" she interrupted.

He smiled at her and shook his head. "We went out a couple times a few years ago, and I eat here a couple times a week."

The waitress arrived. "Can I start you off with some drinks and appetizers?"

"You want a big girly drink?" he asked her.

Hannah shook her head, no, she did not want a girly drink whatever that was, she wanted to know about Remmie and Hawk! "Iced tea please," she said.

He ordered the same and a combo platter of appetizers.

"Couple of times? What does that mean?" she probed. Why did she care? She didn't care. Did she? Of course not, that would be silly. She needed to not ask anything else about it, or he would think she did. When she didn't. Why hadn't she ordered that big girly drink?

Luckily, their tea arrived and she took their entrée orders and left again, promising the appetizers soon. Hannah deliberately changed the subject. "Have you always lived here in town?" Had she already asked him that before? It didn't matter.

Derrick nodded. "Born in the hospital down the road, graduated high school here, attended the community college while I was working for my uncle. How about you?"

"Grew up in St. Peters, Missouri, lived there until I want to college in Maryville, then came home and went to work for an insurance company until I found this hardware store for sale. I always thought I'd take over Dad's when he retired. I grew up in the shop and just loved it there."

"Why didn't that work out?" he asked her, picking up a small quesadilla from the appetizer plate.

"My dad ended up losing it over my mom's health while I was in college," she said. That was vague enough and true enough.

"That had to be hard," he said. "Especially since you'd set your life goals on it."

"It was," she admitted. "Hard on Hunter too. Not to mention our folks who were in a crisis financially, emotionally and physically."

"How are they doing now?" he asked, his dark eyes seemed probing and she shivered. Why? His mere presence and what he did to her.

She shrugged. How were they doing? Her mom's life revolved around doctor appointments and her dad's about worrying about how to pay the bills and going to his GA meetings. "Hanging in there," she said. He shot her a look as she dipped a nacho into a delightful salsa. She'd have to find out if they sold bottles of this.

"What are you going to do when Jer graduates in January and moves?" she asked him while they ate their entrées. She never made Mexican for herself at home, something she needed to change, once she learned to cook.

"Walk around the house in my underwear," he said.

Hannah choked on her taco salad. Yeah, that image was now seared into her brain. But he was standing at her sink, weirdly, looking just fine in low slung jeans, she needed to think of something else. Taking a sip of tea, she looked at his amused grin as if he knew exactly what she was thinking.

"I don't know," he said. "I've never lived alone. I stayed with the folks until Jer's mom and I got an apartment, then I've had Jer ever since. He's spent the night with friends and his grandparents once in a while, but you always know he's coming back. Do you like living alone?"

She shrugged, twisting a piece of her blonde hair around her finger. "I don't mind it. I'm usually too busy to realize I'm alone, and honestly, I never get lonely. There are so many people at work to deal with, some quiet and not having to talk is a relief."

Derrick nodded. "I understand that, though I don't have to interact as much as you do."

"Dessert?" the cheerful waitress asked, as she removed their plates a few minutes later.

Hannah shook her head and pulled out her cell phone to look at the time. "I open tomorrow, I'd better get home," she said to him.

"Store doesn't open until 8 a.m.," he said.

"True, but the boss has to be there by 6 a.m. to get things ready," she said. "Tomorrow is truck day, and on truck days it's 4 a.m."

"How often does the truck come?" he asked as he paid the bill and they walked out to his fancy car. The evening air felt soft and she could feel the beginning of fall in the air. It wouldn't be here for a while though, and she couldn't wait for her first Christmas in her new house and in her new store. She would put a tree by what Hunter called the waste of space corner and she called the gathering spot. Invite people to purchase gifts for the kids in need in town and put them under it. Maybe a small wrapping center, she had so many ideas and she couldn't wait to implement them. She thought about kissing Hawk under the mistletoe as he opened the car door for her and helped her into the car. Kissing Hawk anywhere, yeah, that thought sparked an interest. He probably thought of her as a friend of Jer's though. Maybe not, he did invite her for dinner. Had it been a real date?

They drove through the quiet town and as if he read her thoughts said, "We do Christmas up big in Macintyre. Christmas walks and house tours, downtown gets all decorated up. It's a magical time of year."

Hannah put her ball cap back on as the wind caught her hair. She hadn't thought of him as a magical kind of man. Someone who would think that way, but she rather liked it. It made him seem a little more approachable. She had butterflies around him and never quite felt comfortable, but she figured that was probably more of a crush thing. She'd had crushes before. They were fun. Especially when you got to see the guy every day or almost every day like she did. Well, while she was having her bathroom done anyway. She refused to think of what happened after.

"Here we are," he pulled into her driveway. "Thank you for having dinner with me, I will see you tomorrow probably after work." There was a streetlight half a house down that bathed them with light. "I'll walk you to the door," he said, getting out. Her heart hammered.

"That's okay," she said, opening her door and swinging her legs out. Standing up, she turned to look at him as he came around. "I'm going to wander around in the backyard a minute. I don't remember if I put up the rake and hose or not. Thank you for dinner and for the company. I'll see you tomorrow after I get off work."

He gave her a long look, and said, "See you then," and got back in his car. She watched him drive away and walked around in the backyard. Yeah, she'd not even gotten the rake or hose—did she even own a rake or hose yet? No. She was just terrified he was going to kiss her. It was too soon or he wasn't going to kiss her and that would have been just as bad. Worse? Maybe.

Wandering out back anyway, to calm down, she looked around in the gathering dusk, lit by a few solar lights Jessie had left.

Her backyard wasn't big, but it was so charming. Jessie had a green thumb and it showed. There were flowers everywhere, in small raised gardens, some vegetables over in the corner, an herb garden she had no clue what to do with over on the side of the house. Something smelled great, but she didn't know what it was or what to do with it. She should learn to cook. Sometime. In the future when her store was up and running well and she was semi-retired. See, a plan.

Walking back around front, she reached in her pocket, and had a sinking feeling. Oh no. She didn't have her key. She was locked out.

Chapter 3

Now what? She walked around the house, checking windows and the back door. Jessie had extra security because of little Sam, she was very protective of that boy. Hannah had been grateful for that when she moved in. Now, wandering around the house looking for a way in, not so much. She couldn't believe she hadn't grabbed her keys. She knew right where they were. This time tomorrow night, she would have hidden a spare key out here somewhere, but that did nothing to help her right now.

She hadn't even given Hunter a spare key yet. The only one who had one was... Hawk. Well, there was nothing to do but to call him. For some reason that gave her a little shiver. He wasn't far away yet, surely. Taking out her phone, she dialed his spare number, not his work number.

"Hannah?" he answered.

"Hawk, hi," she said, feeling foolish. "I seem to have locked myself out of the house, and you are the only one with a spare key. Would you mind..."

"On my way," he said.

Sticking her phone back in her pocket, she walked to the backyard and picked a couple flowers for him. Peace offering.

He arrived just a few minutes later. She walked over, for some reason feeling a little apprehensive, but he smiled at her. "I'm sorry, Hannah," he said.

"What are you sorry about?"

"A gentleman always makes sure the lady makes it inside and I failed you. It won't happen again." He took her hand as they walked to the front door and she felt safe and protected.

"I'm the one who said it wasn't necessary," she protested.

"I'm the one who knew better," he said, letting go of her hand to unlock the door.

"Thank you," she said, softly.

He reached under her chin and tilted it so she looked into his eyes. They looked very serious. "You get that key done tomorrow, you understand? You don't want this happening again."

"I will," she promised. "Thank you for coming to let me in. I'm glad I gave you a key."

"I'm glad you did too, not often a man gets to play knight, you know," he smiled at her this time, and she felt that wave of whatever it was wash over her again. Her knees felt weak and she grabbed the doorknob for support. It fell open and she stumbled. Derrick reached over and grabbed her arm, pulling her toward him.

"Whoops," she giggled. "Making a real good impression, aren't I?"

He pulled her further, into his arms for a hug. "Yeah, little girl, you are."

With that he released her, swatted her butt playfully, and said, "Make sure you lock that door behind you."

"Yes, sir," she said, stepping inside the door, and shutting it behind her. Smiling, she rubbed her bottom where he'd smacked her. It hadn't hurt, but she'd felt it. Why did she fantasize about more? She didn't. The idea of going over his knee made her shiver but not in a bad way. It felt more... comforting? That was silly. Of course it didn't. It would be embarrassing and humiliating and probably painful. Right? It wasn't something she would ever want. Besides, she was a strong independent woman, a business owner who just bought her own house. Moved to a new town to start a new life. She didn't need the strength or comfort or even the daddy issues of an older man in her life. Well, he wasn't that much older, was he? He was probably, well, Jer was nineteen, she knew that because she'd done his paperwork when he was hired. So if Derrick was eighteen when he was born, that made him late thirties/early forties. She was twenty-six. That didn't make him an older man. Just mature. Why was she justifying anyone's age? It didn't matter and she needed to go to bed. Alone. So she could get up and go to work in the morning. Because that is what strong, independent women did. They didn't snuggle down on their pillows and dream about being spanked, then her tears kissed away by a Matthew McConaughey look alike, no they didn't. They dreamed about shelves that needed stocking and money that wanted counting while their cat purred on the pillow next to them. Weirdly, her dreams didn't agree.

Heart hammering so hard, she swore the next-door neighbors could hear it, Hannah let herself into the house the next afternoon. Work had been routine and she liked that in a day. Fairly busy, no real crisis she couldn't handle and she'd even managed a few pleasant minutes with her brother when they changed shifts. He'd been busy lately and they almost always worked opposite shifts. When he was off work, he was always off on his boat. He called himself a river rat, he loved being on the water. Fishing, boating, water skiing, he didn't care, he just loved the water. She thought it was okay, but couldn't see the attraction he obviously did. She liked an ocean wave once in a while, but this lake, Lake Constance, just sat there. It didn't do much of anything, but Hunter was in love with it. She was glad he had a passion. Hers was the store and now, her house and maybe the hot guy working on her remodel who called her little girl and threatened to paddle her bottom.

Hearing reno noises coming from her soon to be bathroom, she headed back that way to see what had been accomplished today. He turned as she came in. "Hey, little girl, let's see that key."

Rolling her eyes at him, she said, "It is in my purse and I put that down by the door."

He crossed his arms and gave her a level stare. "I'm waiting."

Shaking her head, and feeling a little, what? Overcome? Flustered? Turned on? What would he have done if she hadn't made the extra key? Would he have spanked her? Well, she had been a good girl and gotten it done. She fumbled for it in her purse, and took it back. "I made several extras," she said. "I gave one to Hunter, one to hide outside and a spare for inside the house, just in case."

"Good girl," he said. "That means you deserve a little shopping trip."

"A shopping trip?" She'd been in a store all day! Besides, most of her shopping was the one-click online kind.

"We need to pick out some cabinets, finishes, back splash and shower tile," he said.

"Oh, fun!" Now, that kind of shopping she could get behind, especially since she wasn't spending any of her real money. "When do you want to go?"

"How about now?" he said, smiling at her in that way that made her go all giddy. What did she like better—little girl or good girl? She wasn't certain.

"I need to go change my shirt first and wash up," she said. "Long day at work."

"See you when you come down," he said. "I'm going to pick up in here for the night."

Was it another date? A first date? Another not really a date?

She didn't care, she was heading out with Hawk again. Yay! Her stomach growled and she frowned in that general direction. "Hush. You will survive another few hours." She hadn't eaten today at work, she'd gotten busy and didn't take her break. She'd have a fit if one of her people did that, for one it was illegal and two, they worked better with a breather now and then. But she was the boss. She could do anything she wanted because she didn't punch a time clock and if working twelve or fourteen hours without a break because it was needed, or she just wanted to, she would be happy to do it for her beloved store. Somehow though, coming home after work lately seemed really important. Well, she needed to check on the progress of her renovation, didn't she? It was only smart. The store would be there when the renovation was over.

Having the reno over suddenly made her sad. That was silliness, she made a face at herself in the mirror as she brushed her teeth and put on some mascara. No one was sad when the mess of renovations was over. They were always pleased and delighted. She would be too.

Or not.

She made another face at her overexcited self, changed into a clean shirt, and went into the other room. "I'm ready," she said as calmly as she could manage.

"Let's go," he said. "Sorry, I don't have Bella tonight, only the truck."

Hannah laughed. "You named your car? Does the truck have a name?"

"Yes, it is Let's Go To Work," he said as he opened the door for her.

"Poor Bella, no middle names," she said.

"She is pretty upset about it. What do you think her middle

name should be?" he asked as he got in on the other side of the truck.

"Shanna," she said without thinking.

"Isabella Shanna," he said. "Why Shanna?"

She was not about to tell him it was the first romance novel she ever read, from her mom's closet shelf. Supposedly hidden. Hot. Sexy. Amazing. She'd been hooked on them ever since. He reminded her of a historical romance hero. Not that she would ever tell him that, of course. "Old friend," she lied. "It's a pretty name."

"It is," he agreed. "Okay, Isabella Shanna Hawk."

Her brain did not go to Hannah Elizabeth Hawk. Nope. She liked Koberline. She never thought about changing it. But, well... Focus, she told herself.

"Hey, we aren't going to my store?" she asked as they drove down the road.

"I get a discount at this one," he said. "We have a working relationship, and you don't carry everything we need."

Well, he had her there. No way they could carry everything this store did. But that wasn't her goal, she reminded herself. She wanted to be a go to destination. Where if someone didn't know how to do something or even what a piece of whatever was, they could come to her store and find help. She didn't want to carry everything. Being the hometown store was more important to her.

"Okay," she said agreeably. After all, she was going out with him. Whatever, wherever. Did she care? Nope. "I can give you a professional discount," she blurted out.

"I'd take you up on that," he told her. "But really, you don't carry most of what I need or in the quantity I need, but I'd be glad to throw as much business your way as I can."

"Thanks, and I'll set you up next week. And, Hawk? Well, I've never picked out backsplash before," she confessed.

"I'll guide you through it," he reached over and squeezed her hand. She smiled, feeling, weirdly protected. She didn't need protected. However... Hannah sighed. Backsplash. Focus.

"You been here before?" Hawk asked as they walked in the huge building. Hannah shook her head. This was nothing like she wanted for her down-home style hardware store. She had been in other, what she knew were big-box stores before, of course, but not this one in this town.

She felt at home though. It smelled like hardware, lumber and tools. Home. A mansion home as opposed to her cottage home, but still.

"Down this way," he told her and she followed him, looking around. They picked out shaker style cabinets in a matte white, and dark black old-fashioned hinges and pulls. The splash above the sink and in the shower were all some sort of subway tile she didn't recognize. They didn't carry that. She knew so little beyond what they had. Something she needed to work on to maybe eventually do an online store with more items than they could carry there. Customer service was their focus. Not here, though, as they wandered around with very little interaction with the staff. But that was okay today, she wanted to be with Derrick anyway and he seemed to know what he was doing, even reaching behind a counter and getting a form to fill out to order the cabinets sent to her house.

Picking out things didn't take nearly as long as she thought—hoped—it would. Next time she would be much less decisive.

"Hawk," a voice purred from behind them. "Introduce me."

Hannah felt him tense up beside her. "Melinda," he said, and slowly turned around. Oh! She was someone! Someone important? She'd find out. Whirling around, she saw an adorable little minx of a woman, she looked like an imp, tiny, long glossy red hair, huge blue eyes. She was either an angel or a devil, Hannah could tell at a glance and her shoes were not from the mall. Well, any mall, she could afford to shop at, anyway.

"Hello, Melinda," Hawk said.

"Who is your woman of the day?" Melinda asked in a tone that Hannah could tell was trying to sound light but failed miserably. One of Hawk's exes? Must be and no reason to be jealous, of course. He had a past. So did she. They weren't dating anyway as far as she could tell.

"I'm Hannah. Hawk and I are here picking out tile for the shower," she said, being deliberately vague.

"Oh, a bathroom renovation." Melinda raked her over and Hannah suddenly felt lacking in many ways, from her mall shoes to her non-salon haircut and her unmanicured nails. She and her bathroom renovation meant nothing to this woman. "Hawk, are you still doing them yourself? I told you ages ago to start hiring those small jobs out."

"Nice to see you, Melinda," he said and began to walk away, but she grabbed his arm, but looked at Hannah.

"You've hired the best," she told her, looking right in her eyes, the other woman's icy blue eyes boring into her as if she knew everything. Knew of her crush, knew what she thought, knew all her desires, and Hannah had to stop herself from shuddering. From what, why? She didn't know, she just knew Melinda was, well, like her first impression, someone. Someone important? To watch out for? Again, she didn't know.

"I've been very pleased so far," Hannah said as sweetly as she could manage.

"I just imagine you are," she said, still clutching Hawk's arm. "I know I was. He did a great job on my," she paused, "renovation."

"References aren't really needed," Hannah said. "I'm a pretty good judge of character. But thank you."

"Goodbye, Derrick Hawk," Melinda said. "Nice bumping into you."

"Goodbye, Melinda." Hannah watched Hawk move his arm away. Her mind raced, and she had a million questions and a million what-ifs and whys. She didn't deserve the answer to any of them, but the biggest question, of course, was if she was a 'reno girl'. He would come in, do a job, romance the homeowner and move on. She wasn't dumb enough to think he asked everyone out to dinner, or threatened to paddle everyone. Or did he? Maybe he did. Maybe that was his game? He didn't strike her as a game player but maybe?

"Oh, I love that countertop for the vanity," she said, deliberately not asking him about her. He was a grown man with a past and that past had nothing to do with her. She had a crush on a hot older guy, life would go on. Right? Right. It would go on, just like he would, apparently.

"It's in the budget," he said.

"Great, we done?" she asked.

"As soon as I turn the tickets in," he said.

They drove home, in silence, her mind racing and she had no idea what he was thinking. He pulled into her driveway and asked, "What time do you work tomorrow?"

"I open again," she said. "You going to be here when I get off?" Well, that sounded a little pathetic, now didn't it?

"I will be," he said. "I'll walk you up."

Oh crap. Her heart sank. She could not believe this. Could not. This never happened to her. Never. Yet twice in two days. She had a pile of keys at home. Inside her locked house and wished she'd thought to hide that key outside like she'd thought about doing earlier. Once again, she hadn't grabbed her purse when she left with Derrick. She had her cell phone in her pocket and always had a credit card and a fifty-dollar bill stashed inside the cover, so hadn't thought of it because she knew he was driving. All thoughts of Melinda fled her head as she looked at Derrick. "Umm." Yeah, that made a lot of sense, didn't it? That grin she adored came over his face, swiftly to be replaced by a stern look.

"Little girl," he said.

She sighed and got out of the car. She was in trouble and she knew it. Nothing to do about it, well, she could lie and call Hunter. He was closing tonight but would run over and unlock the door for her if she called him. Or she could 'fess up and take her medicine' and frankly, that option excited her to her toes. Would he? Dare he?

She stood beside the car, crossed her arms and looked at her shoes. "Umm," she repeated. See how smart she could be?

"Hannah," he said, and lifted her chin to make her look at him. She didn't want to do that, a whole entire lot.

"Yes, sir?" she asked feeling all fluttery and nervous and weirdly, a little turned on. Fine, a lot turned on.

"You forgot your keys." It wasn't a question; it was a statement of fact. She couldn't nod, because he had her chin in his hand.

"True," she managed, feeling her knees tremble. Her chin shook a little too, why?

"Hannah, Hannah, how am I going to help you remember your keys?" He let go of her chin and unlocked the door for her. "Come on, let's get this fixed."

What did he mean? "You, little girl, need some corner time while I'm getting this handled," he said.

Corner time? What was corner time? Well, she knew what corner time was, but she wanted, no, she didn't want, well she thought he was planning to spank her. Had she forgotten her keys on purpose to see if he really would? No, it had been a real accident.

"There you go," he said, and pointed over to a boring corner of the living room, next to the fireplace she loved so much. "Nose in the corner while I fix your key situation." Hannah opened her mouth, then shut it again.

"Right now, hands behind your back, at your waist, now move."

Umm, okay? Then what?

She still felt weirdly turned on, and weirdly wanting to do what he told her to do. What if someone looked in a window or something and saw her standing in the corner like a naughty toddler? Who would do that? Well, no one. Her house was set back from the road and fairly private. No one was going to be wandering by, peeking in her windows. She heard the front door open, but didn't look around, and studiously kept her nose in the corner like she was told to do. What was she supposed to do here in the corner? Contemplate her transgressions, she guessed. Worry about what he was doing behind her? Yeah, she was doing that too. Wonder why she forgot her keys twice in two days when she hadn't forgotten her keys in literally years? It was his fault. He made her ditzy. Ditzy blonde. She was anything but that, unless he was around.

He walked back through the living room on the way to the being-remodeled bathroom she guessed, then came back through again.

"If you belonged to me, little girl, you'd be standing there with your pants down by your ankles," he said on one of his trips back through.

"What?" Did she say that out loud? She hadn't meant to, and her mind raced at that thought and her knees trembled so badly, she thought she'd fall and felt a little glad for the security of the walls on either side of her.

The idea of standing there with her pants at her ankles, her bare bottom on display for him, waiting to be spanked, the entire thought made her dizzy. She couldn't swallow and her mouth was so dry, she thought she'd choke.

The sound of the hammer made her jump. What was he doing? Had he gone back to working on her bathroom and forgotten she was there? How much longer was she going to be standing here? Well, she wasn't being held there by force. She could leave any time. Just turn around and walk away. Yet, she didn't. The door opened and shut a few more times and she began to fidget. Corner time was very boring. She didn't like it and she wanted to know what he was doing.

Finally when she thought she couldn't do another minute, he came into the living room and said, "All right, come here." Was he going to spank her now? Maybe? Did she want him to? No. Of course not, that would be silly. Ridiculous even.

"We got your problem fixed," he said. She looked up at him, trying to blink back strange tears that had no reason to be there.

He took her by the hand and she felt, what? She didn't know how she felt. He walked her to the front door, opened it and showed her where there was a key stashed in a small container in the huge big planter Jessie had left there. They went back inside and there was a new fancy hook and from it hung a wicker basket, she assumed was for her keys. Then he led her to the back door and there hung one of her spare keys.

"When you come in, you hang your keys up first thing," he said. "That way you will see them when you walk out."

That was thoughtful of him. "Thank you," she said, fighting the overflowing feeling of disappointment. She'd really thought, well, that he was going to, well—Darn.

He smiled at her as if he knew what she was thinking. Did he? "You are welcome," he answered. "Did you need a couple reminders on your seat of correction, too?"

Well, that was a convoluted way of asking, she thought, and blushed wildly. Could she? Dare she? She tried to look down at her feet, but once again, he lifted her chin to make her look at him. She didn't want to look at him. How could she turn down the opportunity though? She'd been thinking of this. Dreaming of it? Literally.

"Maybe," she managed to squeak out as she shut her eyes not to look at him. What was wrong with her? Grown women did not want to be spanked, right? Especially not for something as silly as forgetting their keys. She'd already done corner time, which was also ridiculous, of course, so she didn't need her seat corrected. However. Part of her craved it, wanted it. Wondered.

"I thought so," he said. "Can't hurt anything but your butt, I imagine, and might do you some good."

Her stomach churned and she wondered what he was thinking and if she would vomit? Some good? What did he mean by that? He took her by the hand and led her to the couch. Hannah felt a moment of sheer and utter panic and tried to pull her hand away from him, but he held her fast, and sat down pulling her over his knee as he sat. "Here you go, all comfortable?" he asked as if it were a real question that needed answered.

She jerked as his hand patted her bottom and he chuckled a little as if it were adorable. She didn't like this position a whole lot and her entire body thrummed in anticipation. "Forgetting your keys and locking yourself out of your own house two days in a row is just unacceptable, little girl. You know that, right?" He emphasized his last word with a smart smack to her bottom and she couldn't help the surprised squeal. He did one more. "The proper answer is yes sir," he told her.

"Yes, sir," she managed. Was this really happening? "Ow!"

"Ordinarily, your pants would be down, because naughty bottoms need to be bare for a spanking and next time..." He smacked her three more times and she jerked and fought the urge to put her hand back. "Next time, your pants will be down and we will have a lesson well learned, do you understand?"

"Yes, sir," she panted, trying not to kick and wiggle. This actually hurt! "Ow! Okay, I'm done now!"

For some reason, that made him laugh again. There was nothing funny about this! "Not quite," he said, and peppered her bottom with stingy smacks that made her wiggle and protest.

"No more! No more!" Her bottom hurt! She felt vulnerable, helpless and no longer turned on, but close to panicked that she had no power. Is this what she thought it would be? Not really, but yeah, sort of, maybe.

After a few more seconds, minutes, hours, decades, she didn't know for sure, she couldn't help it but her hand flew back and he caught it, giving the tops of her thighs a few smacks and then she suddenly found herself off his lap and down on her knees beside him. Reaching back, she rubbed her stinging burning bottom and looked at him, noticing she had a few tears, when he reached down to wipe them away with his finger. She hadn't noticed she'd cried.

"What do you say?" he asked her.

"That hurt!" she said.

"After a spanking, it's important to say what lesson you learned," he said, wiping her cheek with his thumb again.

"I learned you spank hard," she whined and sniffled.

"Little girl, that was nothing. Next time, you will get the full treatment," he said. "Now, what else did you learn?"

She needed this to be over. "Not to forget my keys," she knew had to be the right answer.

"Good girl," he said and pulled her into a hug. Okay, this part of the spanking she liked. Following her instincts, she climbed up on his lap and nestled close to him.

"That's right, or what happens?"

"I can't get in my house," she said, practically.

"Yes, consequences." He kissed the top of her head, and she turned so he could kiss her lips instead. Yeah, now those were consequences she liked.

Her bottom heat faded to a warm glow as she snaked her arms around his shoulders and pulled him closer to her. Yum. Kissing him felt like coming home after a long vacation, warm, inviting, relaxing and just right. She could do this all day. He could pick her up and carry her into the bedroom if he wanted.

He didn't want apparently, but looked in her eyes. "You okay?"

Was she? She wanted to be kissed more, she wanted cuddled more, she wanted more. "Yes, sir?" she said, tentatively. Was that what he wanted?

"That was just a little warm up," he told her. "Next time will be different, I promise you."

What did different mean—and next time? She didn't want more! Well, at the time she didn't, but right now, she kind of sort of maybe did. How would that be? How could she handle it? Had it hurt as much as she thought? She snuggled closer to him. "Yes, sir," she said again. For the what, hundredth time today? She actually liked saying it to him, Hannah decided. It made her feel, well, she didn't know what. Safe? Something. Whatever this feeling was, she liked it.

"Need some more time in the corner to contemplate?" he asked her.

"I was supposed to be contemplating?" She giggled. "No one told me the rules."

"Why did you think you were there?" he asked as if he really wanted to know.

"I don't know. I didn't think about it, I just did it," she said.

"Well, now you know for next time," he said.

She pouted, looking up at him. "I didn't like corner time. It was boring."

"You aren't supposed to like punishments." He kissed her again and she thought her nerves would zing through her skin. "But sometimes they are needed. I don't imagine you will forget your keys again, will you?"

"No, sir," she said. Well, probably not anyway.

Chapter 4

Hawk unlocked the door to Hannah's house. What was going on with her? Her brother, Hunter had just called him and said she had been so upset about something, he'd sent her home and was working her shift. And that she'd actually gone home. They both knew she had a lot of plans for the store and was redoing planograms all this week. Her going home early, meant she was upset about something or not feeling well and either way, he needed to take care of her.

They'd been dating almost three months now, and he was looking forward to spending the holidays together. Thanksgiving would be coming up in about two months, and while she kept telling him that the next months would be long hours at work, he didn't really think a hardware store had a Christmas rush. Or did they? He hadn't paid much attention to holidays the last few years but now that he had Hannah… or did he have Hannah? What was wrong with her?

"Hannah?" he called as he came into the house. There were her keys, hung up on the hook he'd installed. He'd given her a good blistering about a month ago when she'd forgotten them again and he didn't think she'd be forgetting them again anytime soon. She'd literally kicked her pants off and did his favorite dance, the one of a well spanked girl who tried to stomp and high step the burn out of her bottom while her hands frantically rubbed her well roasted cheeks. Then he'd stood her in the corner for a while to calm down before he let her back into his arms where she'd sobbed her contrition and he'd taken her to bed. He'd been wanting that since the first time he saw her, but who would have thought she'd want him? He had a kid and was sixteen years older than she was. Yeah, that wasn't that much but still. They'd been together almost every night since. He'd noticed the last week or so, she'd been edgy and antsy and he'd been considering paddling the stress out of her soon. Obviously, he was too late if Hunter was calling him to check on her. He should take better care of his girl.

He'd only met Hunter a handful of times, had gone on a boat ride with him and some girl named Annebelle that Hunter didn't seem interested in. They had a good time, and he liked Hunter and was glad Hunter liked him well enough to call him to come check on his sister if she needed it. That was what family was for.

"Hannah!" he called out again. Not in the kitchen, living room or bedroom. He strode to the very recently finished powder/laundry room and found her, curled up on the floor, sobbing her heart out. Was she sick? What had happened?

"Hannah?" He took a few very long steps toward her and sank to the floor. "Little girl, come here, let me hold you," he pulled her into his arms, up onto his lap while she cried so hard he didn't think she could catch her breath. "What's wrong, baby? Talk to me." He patted her back and spoke gently to her, waiting for her to calm down. No one could cry forever, could they? Of course not. He would just wait. What else was he doing?

"Can you tell me what's wrong?" he asked, when her sobbing slowed to a slow whimper.

She shook her head violently and started crying again. Great.

"Hannah, you need to calm down or I'm going to give you something to really cry about." Well, that line might have worked on other generations, but it didn't work on her. Her arms grabbed him around his chest and he thought he wouldn't be able to breathe. The woman was going to choke the life out of him.

Shifting on the floor, trying to get comfortable, he spied something on the edge of the vanity he'd recently installed and caught his breath.

Oh.

Well, oh.

He shifted her to one side and reached up on the end of the counter and pulled it down, holding his breath.

Negative. Her pregnancy test was negative. Was that why she was crying? Why was she crying?

"Hannah, talk to me," he commanded. She buried her head in his shoulder and cried harder. "Little girl, do you need a spanking? I'm here for you, baby," he hugged her as tightly as he could, pulling her close as she continued to clutch him. He'd happily give her whatever she needed right now, but he had no clue what she needed or why.

Derrick could never remember feeling this helpless in his life. What was going on? He didn't know, didn't understand, he just knew this woman, his woman, was in deep grief and he didn't know what to do about it.

If she needed spanked, and he'd found out over the last few months, she often did, he would do it, despite her tears. How? Logistically, it would be challenging with both of them sitting on the floor, but for her, he would do it. If he had to, but all he wanted to do was hold her and comfort her.

This woman had crawled into his heart, somehow, someway. He didn't quite understand it. She was closer to Jer's age than his, but he adored, no, he loved her. He did. They had only gone out a few months, but she was everything he had ever wanted. Hard working, ambitious, yet, quite submissive with him while still having a challenging spark to her. He didn't, couldn't think of anyone who had fit with him better. He hoped they would get to know each other better the next few months and then maybe move in together when Jer left for school in January. Then something more, soon after that. This was right. At his age, he had finally found the right woman for him and she was sitting on his lap, and his leg hurt and she would not stop crying. How could he help if he didn't know why she was upset?

"Hannah, tell me what is wrong, right now or those pants are coming off and you are going over my knee," he said as firmly as he could. Was this the right approach? He hoped so.

His pretty, blonde, blue eyed girl looked up at him, nose red from crying, eyes and lips swollen and told him, "Baby."

His breath caught and he looked again at the negative sign on the test. She was not pregnant. Had she been? He'd used condoms. Sure, they weren't foolproof, but still. Had she lost a baby? Had a miscarriage? Could she have been pregnant and he didn't know? How could she not tell him? His head spun, and he moved her from his lap, stood up, then picked her up and carried her into her bedroom.

He put her on the bed they often shared and watched her burrow into the pillows, covering her face, her little shoulders shaking in sorrow, grief, something. He hated this. What should he do? Finally, he simply kicked off his work boots, climbed in bed with her and spooned her closely while she sobbed. She had to stop sometime. She had to. It was a law. Finally, what seemed like an hour later, she sobbed herself to sleep without saying a word.

He rolled out of bed and went to the kitchen. She would need to eat when she woke up. What was going on? Had she been pregnant? She was twenty-six, of course she wanted a baby. He'd raised a kid already. Did he want to do it again? He hadn't even thought of it. He looked in her refrigerator and frowned. She needed to live off a little more than frozen meals and eggs.

When they lived together, he would make sure to... what? Could they live together? How? She loved her little house. She probably wanted a baby. His kid was going off to college. They were in a whole different place in their lives.

He stopped and put his head in his hand. What if she'd lost his baby? That broke his heart, just thinking of it. Thinking of her losing a baby and carrying one, he sighed. The first killed him, the second terrified him. Another couple of decades of raising a child. Could he? Would he? Yes, to both. Did he want to? There was that, now wasn't there? So what had happened? Whatever it was, obviously affected her a lot. More than a lot. He'd seen and heard her cry before but never like that.

Comfort food. What was comfort food? Mac and cheese? Meatloaf? Pancakes? He didn't even know her comfort food. How could he have a baby with her? Think of forever with her? Of course, he'd dated in the past. Nothing was ever serious though. He hadn't thought of remarrying. He had a kid to raise and a business to build. Those had been his priorities. Had been. He sat down in a kitchen chair. This was a little overwhelming.

He straightened up, but it was nothing he couldn't handle. Whatever worked out, the little blonde in the other room was worth it. He picked up his phone and ordered pizza. Pizza was everyone's comfort food and he'd take her grocery shopping later on. Fill that fridge and pantry with some decent food. Then he went into the living room and turned the TV on to the game. He wasn't leaving until they talked and if that was tomorrow, then it was.

Hannah stretched under her covers. She didn't remember going to bed. How had she gotten here? Oh, yeah, Hawk had come and found her. Tears sprang to her eyes again. Why was she so upset? It was stupid and now she was going to have to explain it to him. Ugh. If he hadn't shown up last night, he would never have to have known anything about anything. Well, she might as well face the music. She got up, took a quick shower, wrapped herself in her soft pink robe, and headed into the living room, noticing it was only ten at night. She'd slept a couple hours but it had been a hard sleep and she felt as if it were morning. Walking into the room, she smelled pizza and saw him asleep on the couch. Why hadn't he come to bed with her? She loved sleeping next to him. With him. She picked up a piece of the not quite warm pizza and took a bite as she settled in the chair across from him.

She was almost done with her slice when he sat up and smiled at her. That was a good sign. "Hey, little girl, you feel like talking?" he asked.

"Can I sit on your lap?" That was where she wanted to be. In his arms, on his lap, being snuggled into the solid feel of his muscles and able to smell his scent. She loved the way he smelled.

"Anytime," he said, patting his lap. Smiling, she walked over and snuggled in.

"I'm sorry," she started.

"For crying? Everyone cries and especially those of the female persuasion," he said, pulling her tighter. "I can handle some tears. What I can't handle is not knowing why."

She appreciated that he didn't mention the elephant of the pregnancy test in the room. But she would have to. Ugh. "Yes, well, I don't cry often," she said.

"Unless you are over my knee getting your little bottom paddled," he teased, gently.

"Oh, hush, that's your fault, not mine," she said. Yeah, she didn't mind those tears. They often felt needed, or cleansing, or something weird she didn't yet understand. "Anyway." She felt him still and had to push herself to say something. "I thought I was pregnant this week. I know we've been using protection, but things happen." He said nothing. So she kept going. "I finally bought the test yesterday and well, I'm not."

"Did you want to be?" he asked and she hesitated.

He just sat there, and waited. "I didn't think I did until I knew I wasn't. Then it seemed like a loss." Did that make sense to him? It didn't to her.

"I'm sorry, baby," he hugged her even tighter until she thought she couldn't breathe. "How are you feeling now?"

"I'm still a little sad, but better. Now isn't a good time for a baby. We just started going out together, and haven't talked about the future at all. The store has been opened less than a year, plus the holidays are coming up, and we know how busy those are." She felt like she was simply rambling, words were coming out of her mouth but meant nothing. So she shut up and waited. His turn.

"I agree with all those reasons," he said. "However, if you were pregnant, that is something we can handle together. It takes two, after all, and one of us two knew nothing about any of this until tonight."

Yeah, she knew that. She hadn't wanted to worry him. "I had nothing to tell you," she said.

"You were worried," he said. He sat back a little and lifted her chin to him so she had to look at him.

"I was worried," she confessed. "I could barely think of anything else all week."

"But you never once told me," he said, slowly. "I've seen you half a dozen times this week. There was an opportunity."

"I didn't want you to worry," she tried. Why hadn't she told him? Because there was nothing to tell. She didn't know anything to tell.

"Hannah, really?" She much preferred little girl or baby to Hannah from him. She'd hurt him, she could tell. "I can handle life. This was a couple problem, not a Hannah problem. I'm upset you didn't tell me." His arms tightened against her. "I know you think I'm going to paddle you and I probably should, but I'm just not. If it ever ever happens again, not just this particular thing, but anything that bothers you, I need to know. I will not be lied to, not by omission or a flat out lie. Do you understand me?"

"I do," she whispered. "I really thought I was doing the right thing by not telling you."

"What do you think now?" he asked.

"I think I was wrong," she said.

"Even without a paddling?" he said, and she relaxed a little. He didn't sound as mad now.

"Yes, sir, even without," she said. Was she disappointed he didn't spank her over this? She deserved it. It always reconnected them, made her feel safe and cared for, in a weird sort of way, and while she didn't like the during, she adored the after. She would have endured the during to get to the after with him. Things just seemed off, somehow. She needed to give him some time. After all, she'd had a week to think on it, and he only had tonight.

"Do you want a baby?" he asked her.

"Well, most people want a family at some point, don't they? How about you? You've already raised a family. Would you want to do it again?"

"I hadn't even thought of it until tonight," he said, and kissed the top of her head. "And I don't think I want to think about it for a while. Let's put the pizza up and go to bed."

Now that she could get behind.

"Hello, I'm looking for those little plastic things that when you hang new curtains the rods stay into the walls." A voice came from behind her and Hannah knew that voice. It was her. From the home store where she and Hawk had picked out cabinets.

Melinda the minx. Melinda the, the what? It wasn't Melinda's fault she didn't like her. Melinda would never know.

"Anchors," she said almost automatically. "This way, I'll show you."

Turning around, she flashed her customer service smile as the other woman's eyes got bigger but for some reason it seemed false. "Oh, I know you!" the red head said. "You're Derrick's latest. I saw you looking at cabinets! I'm Melinda."

"Hawk is remodeling my bathroom, yes," Hannah said as coolly as she could. "The anchors are this way." She led the way down the aisles. His latest? Was Melinda a before? Did she care? Should she? Of course not. They both had lives before they met. If they didn't, both of them would be strange. Adults should have a past. It made them human and normal, she'd already thought all this until she was sick of thinking it, and man, she didn't like this woman.

"I just love coming here. I always get such good service," Melinda said. If she'd been in here before, then it had been when she was off, Hannah knew. She would remember her. She doubted many people forgot Melinda.

"That is always good to hear," she said, though, keeping on her best customer service voice. "We appreciate knowing that. Do you know how many you will need?"

"Oh, give me a couple dozen," she said.

"Sure thing," Hannah said, then asked, because it was part of her job, not because she cared, "Do you know how to use them?"

"Oh, I'm not doing it, I just told the guy doing it I would grab them for him today. He hung the rods about an inch too high and I need him to move them to the proper spot." She flipped her shiny red hair back and leaned in closer. "He isn't as good as Derrick, but he's pretty booked up right now."

"He finished my remodel a while ago," Hannah said, though she didn't have a clue why. It was none of this woman's business.

Why did she feel guilty about hogging his time? She didn't. That was ridiculous. If he wanted to be with Melinda he would be. He wanted to be with her.

"So, tell me, are you one of Derrick's remodel girls?" She peered into her eyes. Hannah didn't think she had ever seen eyes that blue before. Colored contacts? Who knew?

"I told you he did my bathroom," she said, trying not to sound annoyed, but she was, oh yes, she was.

"Oh, you know that wasn't what I meant," Melinda said. "I meant, did he take you out to dinner, date you, spend the night, do a few kinky things?"

Hannah felt her mouth go dry and controlled her breathing by sheer force of will. She bagged the anchors as calmly as she could and wrote the number and price on the bag. "I have no idea what you are talking about," she said. "Here you go. Hope your new curtains look great."

"Oh, they will," Melinda said. "I hire people to make sure of that."

"That's the way to do it," Hannah agreed, hoping she would leave soon.

"Well, you take care of yourself," Melinda's eyes bored into her again and Hannah felt chilled.

"You, too," she said cheerfully. "Thanks for your business."

"I'm always excited about helping out the mom and pop stores," Melinda said. "I know what it is like when you are struggling." With that she swept toward the register and even though she didn't have a cape or a tiara, there was something queen like about her. Or just obnoxious. Hannah didn't know which. But she carried herself well. Hannah thought she had confidence, but she knew her type. They were born into money and privilege and felt people who didn't have it were less than. She doubted seriously Melinda had a clue what it was like to struggle. She seemed the type born into comfort and who just expected it. She figured

Hawk not wanting her was the worst thing that had every happened in Princess Melinda's life

While she straightened and stocked shelves that night, Hannah kept thinking. Could she imagine Melinda over Derrick's knees kicking and crying like she did? No, not really. Is that what she meant by kinky? It had to be. Had he spanked everyone he ever dated? Remmie from the Mexican restaurant he took her to eat? Melinda? His ex-wife? Was that why she had left?

Getting home a little later, she called out, "George? Where are you, kitty kitty?" She needed a hug. He was the most stand-offish cat she'd ever known, but she loved him. He came to the door, looked at her and then stalked off. She watched him go and sighed. Whatever.

Should she call Hawk? No. Last thing she needed was to talk to him now. She was mad. She felt hurt. Used? Maybe even that, too, and her cat wasn't even going to play nice. Men. Had he been using her? Was this his MO? Get a job and have sex with the homeowner? How many other women had he done that with?

It was two more days before she saw him again and by that time she was fuming. He was coming over to take her out to dinner, they had texted earlier and set it up, but she had zero interest in going out to dinner. She'd talked to Jer and he told her that his dad was working for the new doctor who just moved to town and was remodeling her offices. He was trying to get them finished before she opened next month. She knew that, but Hawk hadn't mentioned that Dr. Bronson was young and female. Coincidence? She did not think so. What if she had been pregnant? What would he have done about it? Was she disposable? Was he waiting to dump her until he bedded the doctor?

Hannah paced around the house. How dare he? She was not someone's side chick or fun time or whatever the term for the person who wasn't in a serious relationship with the one she was sleeping with but didn't know she wasn't in a serious relationship with them. Well, stupid. That was a good term, she guessed. Grabbing her hairbrush, she attacked her hair. It wanted brushed. It had gotten long and she needed to go get it cut. But Derrick liked to run his fingers through it and thought it should be longer. She had been on board with that but now? How long was Remmie's hair? Melinda's was past her shoulders, way past them. Should she look at every woman in town with long hair and wonder? Why yes, yes, she should! Why shouldn't she?

She paced around some more. Should she change out of the shorts and tee shirt she'd changed into after work? No. How long was the doctor's hair and should she look again in a month or two? Yes. She was not a throw away doll. Was that even a thing? A throw away doll? Where had that even come from? She didn't know and was working herself up into what her mom used to call a tizzy fit. She was ready to have a tizzy fit. She had real feelings for Derrick Hawk – she'd thought she was having his baby for a week! That was real! How more real could it be? But he, apparently, had real with other people and that not only broke her heart but infuriated her. She wasn't a casual sex kind of person and had no desire to be led on and have him pretend she was important to him. If she was, he needed to prove it. If not, she needed to walk away.

She was having it out with him, as soon as he showed up. She was so over this. So over it. She was no one's toy, no one's plaything. She might be blonde and little but she was not a pushover or a reno girl or a toy to be discarded once he moved on to someone shinier and newer.

A few minutes later, Hawk knocked, then walked in, using his key. Did she need to get her key back? Probably. She would see. He looked tired, but good, as always. Well, she was tired, too. He wasn't the only one who worked.

"Hey, little girl, I missed you," he opened his arms and she hesitated, but the physical longing for him overcame her better intentions, and she went in for a hug. That didn't mean he was off the hook, though. Oh, no, it did not.

"Mmm, I've been needing the feel of you in my arms." Was that his go to line?

"Am I just a remodel girl? Do you say that to everyone?" That didn't come out as sternly as she wanted it to. It sounded a little pathetic, actually.

"What?" Apparently this wasn't the greeting he was expecting.

"Are you using me because you know I think you are hot and smart and all that? You thought I'd be easy?"

"What? Where is all this coming from?" He tilted her chin to make her look at him. "Are you okay?"

"No, I'm not okay." She stepped back and crossed her arms and glared at him. "I hear things, you know."

"Hear things? What are you talking about?" He looked genuinely confused and she almost felt bad for him, but the idea of him with other women and just using her... well, the idea of him touching and hugging and loving other women, just, ah, there was that mad. It flooded over her. She had been falling in love with him, if she wasn't already. What did he feel? That he wanted sex and she was blonde and little and not ugly?

"Are you using me? Am I just a remodel girl? Do you sleep with all your single clients?" Her heart hammered and she felt her hands tremble and her chin quiver. She would not cry. Would not. Firmly biting the inside of her cheek and forcing her fingernails into her palms she looked into his eyes. His eyes made her melt. Were they lying eyes?

"What?"

"That is not an answer."

"Are you asking me if I dated before I met you? Yes, I have. You've dated before me. We'd be weird if we were both celibate virgins, you know."

He took her arm and walked her into the living room and sat

them both on the couch. Why did she go with him? She didn't want to go with him. She wanted to kick him out of her house, after she told him what for and how to and then never speak to him again, right? Well, not really. Maybe.

"No, that is not what I'm asking you. Don't be obtuse." She shrank back over into the corner of the couch and grabbed a pillow and put it in front of her. "Am I a remodel girl?"

"What the hell is a remodel girl?" he asked, looking legitimately frustrated.

"Don't be stupid," she said. It was hard to be mad sitting down. She needed to stand up, yet she didn't. "A client you sleep with while you are working on her remodel and then dump."

"Do I look like I dumped you?" he asked. "Your bathroom has been done for a couple weeks now, and here I am, showing up to take you out to dinner."

"Because I'm a sure thing and you know you can get laid at the end of the evening?"

"Hannah, you may not know it, but you are hurting me right now. You need to watch your words." He looked fairly upset, but so was she, and her feelings counted too.

"No. I won't watch my words and how dare you tell me to! I can say anything I want to say, anytime I want to say it and if I want to know where I stand with you, I can darn well ask!" Watch her words? What kind of crap nonsense was that? "You are not the boss of me!" How mature was she? Amazing.

He stood up and started walking toward the front door. Good! That was what she wanted! She wanted him to leave and go hang out with the doctor woman who had probably already locked herself in her room, chanting 'grow hair, grow!' in order to impress him.

"Don't let the door hit you on the way out," she said. Was he really leaving? Just like that and it was over? She had been right. He wouldn't leave her if she meant anything at all to him. But that was what men did apparently, walked away from you.

"Please, don't." The words slipped out, she hadn't meant them to. But he'd heard them obviously, because he stopped walking to the front door and turned to the bedroom. Oh, she was so not sleeping with him! She didn't care what he thought. Mad sex? Was that a thing? Well, she could see it, but she didn't want it. He came back out, carrying her hairbrush and she stood up and backed away as he got closer, while still clutching her pillow. "No."

"You going to drop the pants or am I going to pull them down for you?" he asked very calmly, as if she hadn't just had a temper tantrum in front of him and as if she planned to let him spank her.

"No."

"That wasn't a yes or no question. I'm going to blister some sense into your cute butt and, little girl, you are not going to be sitting comfortably for the next week."

"No." She kept backing away until her back hit the wall. Why had she gotten a stuck-up cat instead of an attack dog? Eyeing the hairbrush she'd been using earlier, she knew exactly what was going to happen and that there was nothing she could do to stop it. Could she? Did she want to? Why didn't her brain ever shut down?

"Don't push for an ass whooping if you don't want one," he said, and reached over, taking her by the elbow and walking her to the couch. Her heart hammered and she felt more vulnerable than she had in her life.

"I'm sorry," she whimpered. "No, I didn't mean it."

"Oh yes, you did," he said. "Don't start lying to me now, because that will make it worse, not get you out of it." He sat down on the couch, and yanked her over his lap. Why was she putting up with this? She wiggled, and tried to get up, but he wasn't having it. His control over her was a little, a little what? "Ow!"

"These shorts are coming down," he said. "And I'm not stopping until you kick them off." Suddenly she needed to pee. Badly.

"Please don't," she whimpered. "I'm sorry."

"No, you are sorry that you are going to get your butt blistered and, little girl, I mean blistered." She heard the smack almost before the heat seared into her bottom.

"You are not a remodel girl, whatever the hell that is." And the hairbrush fell five more times. Why was she counting? What else did she have to do. Should she try and take it? Yes. But...

"Ow, Hawk! No more!" That hairbrush hurt. Sure, he'd spanked her before, but always with his hand. She didn't like the hairbrush. She didn't like the fact he yanked her shorts down. She howled as the hairbrush came down again. "No more! Please!"

"Remodel girl." He smacked her twice more and she started to cry. The pain in her bottom hurt, but mostly his tone made her cry. "The fact you think I lied to you." Down came a flurry of smacks and she didn't think she could take it. "I don't lie."

"I'm sorry!" she sobbed out, but knew it wasn't going to matter. She knew she was kicking and twisting and sobbing and still he didn't stop. He had both her wrists in one hand and that horrible hairbrush kept coming down. It was awful. It was never going to end and he was going to spank her butt off, she just knew it.

"No more, no more, I'm sorry," she sobbed.

"If you can still talk, you aren't sorry enough," he said, and redoubled his efforts it seemed. Shrieking, she kicked and twisted, trying to get away, but he kept hold of her firmly and continued his efforts. He was going to kill her, she just knew it, there was no way she could take any more of this and live. Why wouldn't he stop? He needed to stop.

Not being able to take anymore, she just collapsed, and tried to catch her breath between sobs. She couldn't breathe. Had he stopped? Was it over?

He stood up, dropping her onto the floor, then grabbed her arm and pulled her up to stand and she noticed her shorts were down at one ankle. Reaching back to rub her burning, flaming bottom, he grabbed her hands and marched her to the corner. No, she needed hugged and held. Not corner time.

Trying to catch her breath, she heard him say, "Hands on your head." What? No, she needed to rub, she needed held. The hairbrush fell twice again, once on each thigh and she danced and figured out what 'hands on her head' meant. "Good. Now you just stand there until I decide I'm calm enough to deal with you and if you step out of place or move your hands you will be back over my knee again so fast you won't know what happened."

He had never done this before and she didn't like it. After a spanking he'd always rubbed her bottom and held her close and petted her and kissed her and they usually ended up making love. She liked that. Well, one other time he had stood her in the corner after, but only for a minute and told her to calm down, not that he had to calm down. She didn't like being put away from him and standing in the corner with her bottom throbbing and burning and her hands on her head and not able to move. There was no way she could take anymore, so she didn't dare move but her bottom needed rubbed so badly and she wanted to dance – wiggle – something – the burn out. How long would this burn last? She hated it. Plus she just needed held and forgiven.

"Hold still," he commanded and she realized she'd shifted as she sobbed. How could he be so mean? Why wouldn't he hold her? Did she deserve to be held? What had been wrong with her? Why had she accused him of what she did? What if he'd said something like that to her? She hated that her probably bright red bottom was just out there and she couldn't pull up her pants or wipe her nose which was running like crazy. She sniffled hard a couple of times while she tried to stop the tears and shudders and sobs.

"I don't know what got into you, but I won't have that kind of nonsense from you again," his stern voice came from behind her. "Do you understand me?"

She nodded.

"Answer me," he said. She couldn't stop crying long enough to talk, could she?

"Ye-es, sir," she managed and broke down in sobs again.

"If you don't want another round of what you just got, you better get that nose in the corner and stand still," he said.

Mournfully, she did as she was told, putting her nose as close as her shuddering shoulders would let her, leaving her hands on her head and feeling as pitiful as she ever had in her life. She hated this. Hated hated hated. Never ever again would she put herself through it.

"I don't know why you think you can have yourself a tantrum with no consequences and accuse me and other people of all kinds of stupid things? That is not who my little girl is and I will not have it. Do you understand?"

She started crying harder. Sobbing consumed her and while she realized he was saying something, she didn't know what. Could she feel any worse? What had she been thinking? Although she tried to do as she was told and hold still, her knees gave way. Sinking down to the floor, she felt as if her world collapsed.

Then she was in his arms.

Derrick scooped her up and carried her to the bedroom. Had he been too rough on her? This crying meant her remorse was real, and he knew he needed to nip this kind of behavior in the bud, but he felt a twinge of guilt. While he was a member of the 'bottoms could take a lot' club, he'd given her a bit more than a lot. Nothing too harsh but she was still new to this.

He pulled the rest of her clothes off and went to the bathroom for some ointment he'd stashed in there for just such an occasion. When he came back, she'd curled up on her side, so he rolled her over on her stomach.

"I'm just going to make you feel better," he said as he smeared the ointment on his hands and applied them both to her hot red little bottom as he felt her jerk, then relax. She would think of him every time she moved for the next few days. He rubbed the ointment in until she stopped her hitched breaths and occasional sobs and started to relax, then put lotion on his hands and started rubbing her back. Nothing like a back rub to make everything better. There was a new task for her, learn massage, he liked a back rub, too. He was getting good at this task thing.

"So you ready to talk?" he asked.

"Yes, sir," she said, softly. "I'm sorry."

"Little girl, I promise you, if I ever decide to leave you, I will be a man and tell you. I'm not going to screw around behind your back. That is not the kind of person I am."

"Yes, sir," she whispered. He could tell she wasn't really believing him, so he rolled her over and started massaging her front.

"With these magic hands, I can get any woman I want, but I only want them one at a time. I don't lie or cheat and I expect the same from you. If you are ever done with me, or interested in someone else you let me know. There won't be a scene. I want both of us to be in this, until we aren't."

He hoped they would both be for a long time. Very long.

Hannah sat up, made a face and shifted on her bottom, then curled her arms around his neck and kissed him. That was what he needed, all right. Just that. And her. He began to peel off his own clothes.

Chapter 5

"Hi, Bronwyn," Hannah greeted one of her friends. "How are things today?"

"Great," Bronwyn looked around and Hannah knew she was looking for Hunter. He was off today. Too bad for both of them. "I was wondering if you were going to Jessie's tonight?"

"I am," Hannah said. "I've not been to a girls' night for a while. It will probably be the last one until the holidays are over. Things are going to get busy here."

"You're lucky. Everyone is going to wait until I'm sitting down to some sort of holiday dinner to spring a leak," Bronwyn said. "It's how life goes, but luckily there is this thing called holiday pay."

"And I bet they are glad to pay it," Hannah said. "Hunter is out on his boat for one of the last times this year, I imagine." She knew Bronwyn wanted to know.

Bronwyn looked disappointed and Hannah fought down her smile. She liked Bronwyn, and hoped she and Hunter would get together. "Hey, I know we are going to Jessie's tonight, but I was wanting to try a new recipe out next week. I was going to invite

Hunter and Hawk, just a little intimate family dinner. Want to come?"

"Only if I can bring dessert," Bronwyn said, looking much less depressed than she did a minute ago.

"Great, next Wednesday, Kevin closes that night, and I'm off. I'll let you know." Hannah smiled at her. Maybe Hunter would notice Bronwyn at her house, if there was no one else there. He had dates occasionally but didn't seem to notice the cute plumber who hung around the store hoping for a glimpse of him. Did she like fishing? Hannah hoped so. Or that she at least liked boats. Her brother would live on his boats if he could, she thought. He had a bass boat and a pontoon boat and was making noises about a rowboat. Seriously? Was he half fish? What was it with him and water? She liked an occasional boat ride sure, but three boats? Whatever. She wasn't in charge of either his money or his time. She loved him, admired his brain, knew he would always be there for her, and couldn't care less what he did on his downtime, just like she doubted he knew what she did on hers. They were close, but not that close. It just felt normal to her. They were family, they were business partners and worked semi-well together, but they didn't live in each other's pockets. However, he would come for dinner next week if or when she asked, there was no doubt in her mind. Was she playing matchmaker? Not really. Bronwyn had a huge crush on Hunter and she thought it was adorable. Hunter needed to settle down. Didn't he?

She smiled and thought of Hawk. They had never double dated, she realized. She wanted him to know her family. They went out, sure, but they had never been a couple in a small social situation. It would be fun, she told herself. Fun. yes.

Wincing as she squatted to face the shelves, she still smiled. Hawk had been hard on her the last two weeks, since the remodel girl incident. She liked it, though she would never tell him that. He had started giving her rules – rules! Tasks, he called them and said she would be getting more. She was a grown adult who had taken care of herself for a long time! But still. She had to text him mornings he wasn't with her, let him know what she was eating and when, snap pictures of what she was wearing, and occasionally, what she wasn't wearing.

Weirdly, the stricter he was with her, the happier she was with him. What was with that? The other night, she had even called him daddy and that had freaked her out until he paddled the freak out of her.

She owned her own business. She paid her own bills. She had her own house. And she had a boyfriend she called Daddy. Ugh. It was weird, right? Or was it? Yeah it was. Or not. No, it really was.

Who knew? Whatever, she wasn't going to overthink it, just enjoy the ride. Sometimes she made herself laugh. Of course she was going to overthink it. That was what she did.

Once in the back room, she stashed her boxes and then slipped her phone out of her pocket and texted Jessie. She hadn't seen her for a while, with her busy life, maybe she and Mac could come for supper too, and see what all she'd done to the house.

Then she texted Hawk a quick hi and got back to work.

Wednesday morning felt like fall, as she got up, stretched and texted Hawk a good morning. She couldn't wait for tonight. He was planning to spend the night after her little party. She wasn't the best cook, but could throw a ham in the crock pot and buy some sides at the grocery store. She headed to the store about an hour later to get things for the party. Hawk had this thing about her eating, insisting she eat a decent meal at least once a day, and he didn't think zapped frozen dinners were 'decent'. He could be annoying but she rather liked that he cared about her. Plus he was a very good cook and she didn't mind turning over some of the meal planning to him. He was filling the small pantry off the kitchen with things he called 'staples' which seemed like a lot of DIY stuff to her. Rice, beans, flour. Really? How often did people actually use those kinds of things? She couldn't remember ever using dry beans in anything. Canned beans sometimes, sure, but never dry. Speaking of beans, baked beans would go well with ham, some potato salad and slaw. There were some pre-packaged rolls she could heat up, and who said she wasn't a good cook? Ha! She'd just made dinner and hadn't even left the store.

Turning the corner, she sighed as she saw a glimpse of very red hair. Melinda. How come she never ran into anyone fun or interesting, like Jason Momoa? Nope, just Melinda and there was something about her that just gave her the… well, she didn't like her much.

"Why, Hannah, fancy meeting you here," Melinda said, pushing her almost empty cart, but for some fresh vegetables in there. Carrots with the green stuff still on it? Why, when they came handily already peeled and chopped in small almost bite sized pieces for you? Who was she trying to impress? Hannah saw Melinda rake her eyes over her packaged salads and turn away. Hannah felt judged, but didn't care. Much. Maybe a little. She shouldn't though.

"Hello, Melinda, did you get your curtains hung?" Hannah tried to stay friendly. Always be nice to potential customers, no matter how you felt about them. That had been hammered into her head as a kid.

"I did, thank you," Melinda said. "I'm working on this little house I have, and was thinking of having Derrick come and build a sunporch for me, but I haven't decided yet the style I want."

So you want to be one of his remodel girls? It was on the tip of her tongue to say, but she bit it, hard. Nope. She was not going there. Not at all. No reason to. "I'm sure he'd do a great job," she said. "I'm very happy with my bathroom remodel."

"Oh, I just know he would," Melinda said. "I wasn't worried about that at all. He's done other work for me, you know."

"Well, I need to run, good to see you," Hannah said, and started pushing her cart down the aisle. Melinda's voice followed her, "Tell Derrick to give me a call next time you run into him."

Oh, yeah, that was high on her list of things she wanted to do, all right. Planning to conveniently forget she ran into Melinda was much higher on her list of things to do rather than tell Hawk to call her. She went to the self-checkout and rang up her groceries and headed out to go home, clean and do what passed, in her mind, as cooking.

Hawk hadn't been here for a couple days and she couldn't wait to see him tonight. He'd been busy, she'd been working, today was her first day off in six days and she was looking forward to puttering around her house. Plus doing her little dinner party tonight. There was Bronwyn, Hunter, Jessie and Mac and of course, Hawk. Her first time using her little dining room for something other than piling things on the table and she had bought a new tablecloth online and couldn't wait to see how it looked. It was all sunflowers and happiness, and she loved it.

Decorating her little house brought her joy, making food, not so much, but, hey, she could pull it out of her hat if she needed to. Going into the bedroom, she changed out of her jeans she'd worn earlier while it was cool and put on a pair of shorts, playfully throwing her jeans on top of George, zonked out on her bed. He pretended not to notice and Hannah turned around to look at the purplish-black bruises on her bottom. Who would have thought she'd like bruises on her butt? Oddly, though, she really did. She still didn't like the during—spankings hurt! She didn't like being so exposed, she didn't like the pain, but if she was being honest, she rather liked the excitement of the anticipation of a spanking before, the zinging nerves, the adrenaline rush, and she loved the after. After was when he held her and comforted her and they cuddled and kissed and most generally he took her to bed. If only there didn't have to be a during where she cried and sobbed and it just hurt.

Pulling up her shorts, she headed to the kitchen to start the ham. She cut open the packaging, made a few slices into it, dumped it in the crockpot then poured a can of crushed pineapple over it, just like her mom used to do it. There. She created the entrée. Grabbing another crockpot, she poured a couple cans of baked beans into it, added catsup, brown sugar and a shake of dried onion. Then she stuck the slaw and potato salad containers into the fridge and left the rolls on the counter to heat up later. Entertaining was easy. She didn't know why she didn't do it more often!

She did need to clean the bathrooms though. It was wonderful to have two bathrooms, even though she was mostly here alone. With George, of course. His litter box needed changed too. She could so be a housewife, she told herself. Putter around the house all day and enjoy life. Well, she enjoyed life at the hardware store, too. It was the only thing she'd really ever wanted to do, and other than a few years working part-time retail in a clothing store, and at the insurance company, it was the only thing she'd ever done. She could see herself retiring from that store in about forty years. Hopefully it would make them both a good income until then. Would Hunter want to stay there that long? She hoped so. It was nice to have a partner. He was actually there a few more hours a week than she was, because she did some of the work from home, bills, schedules, ordering, payroll. They would need to hire someone else, or two someones to work over the holidays with them. That was Hunter's job but she needed to see if he'd started looking yet. It was September already and time was getting close. Jer was leaving in January for state college so they would probably keep at least one of them on after the holidays. It would be nice to need a few more people, soon. Their business was building slowly, but it was definitely building, and she was excited. This was actually, she thought guiltily, even better than taking over their dad's business. This one was all theirs.

Oh, did she need wine or something? She rarely drank so generally there wasn't any in the house. Well, that's what a boyfriend was for, now, wasn't it? She shot him off a quick text and realized a little guiltily she hadn't eaten yet today. Well, she'd be having her decent meal this evening, surely that would be sufficient. She'd snack later when she got hungry.

Hawk texted her back a quick, "Okay," and she smiled. He was busy, trying to finish up the doctor's remodel by the end of the week, often working fourteen-hour days which was why he hadn't been over. He'd been beat. But tonight he would be and maybe she would be? Who knew? Not her. Nothing she had any control over, mostly.

She continued cleaning and then went outside to what she still thought of as Jessie's garden, because she hadn't done anything with it at all, and picked some late flowers for the dining room table. She would pick Jessie's brain next spring for ideas to do with it. She didn't have a green thumb. She had a hardware brain. That was all she needed to have.

She put the flowers in a small vase she'd had for a while, and put it in the center of the table. Nice.

She picked up her ringing phone from the counter. "Hawk! Hi! Good morning, no, it's afternoon, isn't it?" She smiled into the phone.

"Taking a quick break and just wanted to hear your voice," he said. "How's my little girl?"

"Missing you," she said. "Can't wait for tonight."

"I'll be there," he said. "I miss you, too. Where was my breakfast picture?"

Hannah sighed. Dang, of course he'd miss it. "I ran out to the store early," she evaded.

"So ten swats for skipping breakfast and ten for not really confessing. Lunch?"

"Derrick!" she whined while that weird feeling shot through her.

"It's early yet, you could eat," he suggested. "Or I could just add ten more."

She shivered. "There are still bruises on my butt from last time," she complained.

"Eat and send me a picture," he said. "Take care of my little girl and I will see you in a few hours."

She smiled as she hung up. Yeah, she would. Feeling a little nervous about introducing him to her brother and her friends, well, they all knew him already but they didn't know them, the couple them. They had gone for a boat ride with Hunter once, but Hunter had been all focused on his boat, of course. Suddenly thinking of Melinda, she wondered if Jessie or Bronwyn would think of her as his remodel girl. Did they know about that? Was it really a thing? Maybe she could find out. Maybe she had no business finding out. Maybe there was nothing to find out.

Hannah shook her head and headed over to the kitchen to get the plates to set the table. She hoped George wouldn't jump up there. Had he ever? Not that she knew. Washing the plates off, all but the top two had been sitting there a while and could be dusty, she tried to push thoughts of Melinda out of her head. What she needed was a good dose of Derrick's hairbrush technique.

Oh, wow. Her knees literally shook at the idea of Melinda over Derrick's lap. No. Just no. He was hers. Starting to giggle, Hannah sank to the floor. Absurd! She was the only one the man could spank, leave bruises on her butt, let her call him daddy. Which had only happened once and she would try not to do it again, but still! He wasn't allowed to bruise anyone else no matter how much they might need or deserve it.

She thought back over the last few months. Her life had changed since Derrick was in it. She was happier, felt more free, more secure, which was silly because she hadn't felt insecure before. She liked his rules and she liked his discipline. Well, liked wasn't the right word, but yet, it sort of was. Weird.

Two days was too long to go without seeing him. Why had she invited people over tonight? It was inconvenient. Maybe he would get there early enough they could have a quickie or something before everyone arrived? She just needed, craved, wanted, desired to be with him.

For how long? Forever? How could she think that? What did he want? It was too early. They'd only been going out a couple months. She rolled her eyes at herself and got out silverware and ripped open a package of paper napkins she'd bought earlier. Usually she used paper towels, but hey, she was all fancy tonight. She finished setting the table and then put the salads in glass bowls and covered them, and put them back in the fridge. See how domestic she was?

She would wait until almost time for everyone to come and then pop the rolls in the oven to warm and smell up the house. She heard his key in the lock, finally!

"You're here!" Hannah threw her arms around his neck and hugged him close, inhaling deeply. She missed the smell of him. He smelled so good, and looked even better in his clean jeans and pressed chambray shirt. The blue brought out the gray in his eyes and she felt proud that he was hers. He was, right? Yes. She needed to stop this insecurity.

"I missed you, baby," he said, "but I'm going to drop the wine and beer if you don't watch out."

"Oh, sorry," she said, feeling as if she were beaming. Two days was too long. She grabbed one of the sacks from his hand and hugged him again with her other arm before, reluctantly, she let him go and walked to the kitchen.

"What can I do to help?" he asked.

"You can sit down and tell me about your day while I ice the beer and refrigerate the wine," she said.

"On schedule and on budget," he said. "Hope to be done by

the end of the week. I have another job starting Wednesday next week, so I might have a couple days off if I can finish."

"A sunroom?" she asked.

"How did you know?" He looked at her with those eyes and she felt a chill.

Melinda. Of course it was.

"Lucky guess?" she said, bending over to put the wine in the fridge and then put the beer in the cooler with ice. It was all cold so should be good when everyone got here in half an hour or so.

"Don't lie to me, little girl," he said in that tone that made her shiver.

"I'm not," she said. "Just saw Melinda in the store today and she said she was thinking of hiring you to do a sunroom. She works fast."

"We set up the contract last week," he said, folding his fingers and giving her that look again. She didn't like that look.

Last week? Well, that wasn't what she said at all now, was it? Had she been trying to get a rise out of her? Make her feel, what? Insecure, threatened? She didn't know.

She took a deep breath and smiled at him. Yeah, she wasn't jealous, insecure, anything. Nope. She was pleased he had another job, of course. That was the name of the game, after all, working for a living, right? Right.

"Have you done sunrooms before?" she asked, calmly as if it were the job that mattered.

"Couple of them. Come here. Give me a hug," he said and opened his arms.

Why did she hesitate? She didn't know. No reason to, just like there was no reason for her to be jealous of a job. She was special to him, she knew. She knew. There was no such thing as a remodel girl.

Right? Right. And right now, she had a dinner party to throw. Throwing her arms around him, she hugged him hard, gave him a kiss and said, "Wanna slice my ham, big boy?"

He smiled. "I do want to slice your ham."

Later that night, she snuggled next to him, exhausted and happy. "I think tonight went very well, don't you?" she said. "I can't believe Jessie is going to have twins. Sam isn't even two yet, she will have her hands full."

"Yeah, Mac needs to learn to keep it in his pants," Derrick said. "That is hard on her. I hope he gives her all the support she needs."

"She looked happy about it," Hannah said.

"Well, of course she did. But three kids under three is a lot. One kid is a lot. I can't fathom doing that."

Hannah thought. He was right. It would be a lot. If anyone could handle it though, it was Jessie and Mac. He was right, it was a lot. Another surge of jealousy came over her and she sighed. "A boy and a girl, they will have a perfect little family." She rolled over on her back.

"Derrick, do you want a baby?" That came out of her mouth before she thought it. But why not. Everyone wanted a baby at some point, didn't they?

He kissed the top of her head. "I've been thinking on that," he said. "Since, well, you know."

Since she thought she was pregnant, yeah, she knew. She kept thinking of it too. Her clock wasn't even ticking but still. She wanted to be a family with Derrick. Raise a kid to take over the store one day. Did he want that? She didn't know. He'd already raised a kid. They had only been going out a few months. Why was she even thinking of this? She knew why. He probably knew why, too.

"And?" She pressed the issue.

"I think it is something we can discuss sometime," he said, and rolled over on top of her again. "And have fun practicing in the meantime."

That would have to satisfy her for now, she guessed.

"Hannah, I'm taking a couple days off," Hunter told her as they unloaded the truck a few days later.

Great. That was what she needed right now. "When?"

"Leaving Saturday and won't be back until Wednesday to work," he said.

She stared at him. "That is more than a couple days and doesn't give me much notice." Oh well, what else was she doing? Rodney and Kevin would pick up another shift or two and she'd work longer days and get the store decorated for fall. She wasn't really a Halloween person, but a lot of people were and she'd get the store ready for their decor and hardware needs. Hawk had started the job at Melinda's sooner than he thought and, of course, he was working long hours. She might as well work.

"Just because I'm all nosy and everything, where are you going?"

"Taking Bronwyn to Lake Michigan for a few days," he said, casually, as if it were something he did all the time.

Hannah stared at him. "Say what?"

"You heard me. Turns out she likes to boat and fish, so we're going up there and renting a fishing boat for a few days."

"You're kidding me, right?"

"Hannah, vacations are a thing, people take them."

"Not with people they've barely met. Not on the spur of the moment." She couldn't believe this. Hunter never did things like that. She'd been dating Hawk for a few months and they hadn't gone away for the weekend yet.

"Apparently it is," he said. "I got that new guy hired part-time, by the way, so he can help you out, and Rodney is always up to taking a few more shifts. I've already told Kevin, and he's cool with it."

"New guy's paperwork on my desk in back?" she asked, trying to shift back to work mode.

"It is, he's coming in this afternoon to go over it with you. I have two more interviews set for next week after I get back so he should be trained before we hire the next one."

She nodded and turned back to look over the planogram she had in her hand but her mind was still on her brother and Bronwyn. She needed to call her girlfriend as soon as she got off work. How come she knew nothing of this? She didn't know they'd even seen each after her little dinner party the other night. Sure, she'd noticed they hit it off well, but hadn't heard from Bronwyn since. No wonder! She'd been busy with her brother! Hannah grinned, well, that would be lovely. She wouldn't mind having Bronwyn hanging around. Hopefully their vacation would go well and they both came back happy.

Starting to pull the batteries off their pegs, she piled them into a small cart and began moving shelves and hooks. Her brain ran while she worked. Derrick and his rules. Now he wanted to give her a bedtime because he thought she didn't get enough sleep. Weird. She was not a child to be put to bed because they were cranky. Yet, other than being a little annoyed, it was also a little thrilling to her for some weird reason, like her required check-ins throughout the day always made her happy and feel secure. Why did she like his rules? They were silly and he warned her that he would be having more for her, and for some reason that excited her down to her toes, but especially places in between. She wanted more rules, more strictness and she didn't know why. She'd probably get tired of them after a while, but for now, it was something new and different, and rather intriguing to her. It had never crossed her mind that she would have a relationship like this. Was it because he was older than she was? He wasn't that much older. Was it because she was weak and needed rules? She didn't think so. It was just odd. She kept trying not to overthink it but overthinking was basically what she did.

All the time.

"I'm unlocking the doors," Hunter called.

"Ready when you are," Hannah called back.

"Me, too," Tonya, their cashier, agreed. "Coffee is ready."

"Waste of space," Hunter muttered as he walked by her and Hannah giggled. She didn't think so. She really liked her cozy little corner with the three rockers, a couple of Adirondack chairs, and the coffee pot set up. The old-fashioned checkerboard and the chatter of the men and occasional woman as they visited. It made the place feel homey. Sometimes, someone brought homemade cookies or bread and shared and she always liked that.

Not as much as she liked Derrick though. He talked about having her take a cooking class. She didn't care about cooking, but he thought she should learn. He said she needed to learn to eat better, and a cooking class would help with that. One of her tasks this week was to do some research and present him with three different options of classes to take. Wonder what he'd do if she didn't? She shivered at the thought. Yeah, willfully defying him wasn't something she wanted to do. She smiled as a woman walked by her, "Hello, I'm Hannah, can I help you find something?" Enough of Derrick, her day had officially begun.

A few hours later, she smiled at Joseph as he sat in front of her. "So you just moved back to town?" she asked as she typed information into the computer. Hunter had already hired him, of course, but she liked to get to know the people working for and with her. "I did," he said. "Looking for a seasonal job to tide me over until my teaching job starts in January. I'll be working out at the college, then, but I like to keep busy," he smiled at her and she couldn't help but smile back. All right then, he was adorable. "I moved back to help take care of my dad, so this job with flexible hours and the perk of getting an employee discount is great. He's let the house go since Mom died and he got sick."

Cute and family oriented. She liked that. Nothing wrong with working with eye candy. "Great," she said. "I'll give you your schedule before you leave today. Hunter is taking a few days off and I've got to shuffle, so I hope you are ready to hit the ground running."

"No problem." He smiled at her and showed perfect white teeth in that smile. "I can handle it."

"If you need specific times off," she said, "we have this really fancy pack of post it notes, and you just write it down and stick it on the board here. I usually do the schedule at least two weeks out but after Thanksgiving, I'll have it for the entire month of December so people can plan their parties and get togethers. So check the board here where it's posted and try to let me know as soon as you can about your needed time off."

"Will do," he said. "Other than the occasional doctor appointment for Dad, and I know those well in advance, I should be good."

"Sounds great, come on and I'll show you around." She swiveled in her chair. "Here are the lockers, you can keep snacks, spare drinks, your cell phone, whatever in there. If you put in anything valuable, you can bring your own padlock for it."

"Can I buy a padlock here, with my new discount?" he asked.

"We'd actually prefer that," she said. "Hooks for coats this winter, mini fridge and microwave if you bring food that needs it. Unfortunately the desk or the card table here are the only places we have to eat, but it works. Breaks are twenty minutes every four hours and if you are here more than six, lunch is half an hour plus a break. And you have to take them, rules are rules."

"Yes, ma'am," he said. "Won't be a hardship."

Hannah giggled. "Glad to hear it. Have you run a cash register before? I'll have Tonya train you on it before she goes today. Usually we only have one open but if there is a line, any of us can jump on the other one and work the line down."

"I'm a quick learner," he said and she noticed he had to be almost six-two. Nice. Well-muscled and not bad at all on the eyes. "Okay, I need you to sign this and we will get started. Hunter is gone for the day, but you will be working with him soon. We will do the cash register training today and then you can head home and be here tomorrow at four p.m. but I'll give you the schedule for the next two weeks before you leave."

"Sounds good, thanks for hiring me, Hannah."

She did a quick store tour and then turned him over to Tonya to train him. She had half an hour before she left for the day, then Jer would be in to close with Rodney tonight. She had a dinner date with Derrick and then hopefully he would spend the night tonight. She hadn't seen much of him since he started to work with Melinda. At Melinda's. Building a sunporch at Melinda's. She was tired of it, and needed some time with him. She wasn't jealous, of course. Why would he give her tasks and rules if he didn't care about her? No reason. He wasn't interested in Melinda any more than she was interested in Joseph. Where had that thought come from? She was being weird today. His fault for not paying much attention to her lately. She craved him more than she could deal with today. Probably because he was coming over, she assured herself. No other reason.

"Hi, Rodney," she greeted a bit later. "How was your day off yesterday?"

"It was good. Heard we hired a new guy," he said, putting his dinner in the refrigerator.

"His name is Joseph," she said, "and Hunter is going to hire at least one more, if not two for the holidays and to cover for Jer when he leaves."

"You mean after he gets back from his trip with the pretty plumber girl?" Rodney asked.

Was she the only one who didn't know? That made her irritated at her brother, not that it would do any good, of course. She might as well not be. His life was his life and hers was hers. They were business partners and while, yes, family, they had their own lives and he owed her nothing about his life any more than she would ever tell him Derrick gave her rules, paddled her butt, stood her in the corner and loved her like a wild man. Yeah, that was a conversation she would never have. He owed her nothing more than an 'I need time off' but next time he owed her a little more notice and they would have that discussion. After she took a little time off when he got back. Just a few days, to play housewife for Derrick.

Dang, she needed to work on looking up those cooking classes later. Nope, not tonight. Tonight was all about spending time with Derrick. Her tasks could come when he was with Melinda. Well, working on Melinda's house. Sunporch. Not being with her.

Going over a few things with Rodney and then sending Tonya and Joseph home, she greeted Jer, and took off. Hopefully Hunter would get on hiring a few more people like he said. They had their workload about even by years of shared responsibilities in the store. Looking back, she realized her father had given her and Hunter much more responsibility than most children had and that gave them both a strong foundation to build from. They worked like a well-oiled team, and even though the store was new, they had fallen right into old patterns.

"I'm out of here," she told Rodney and Jer who were going over the night routine. "Call me if you need me."

"Tell the old man hey from me," Jer said and she jerked her head. They had never discussed her relationship with his dad. It made her feel a little wonky, to be honest. She guessed at some point, she should talk to him about it, but not now. Now she wanted to go home and take a shower and put on something clean, fresh and a little revealing for Derrick. She sighed and waved at him as she walked out the door toward her car. The coffee drinkers had all gone home for the day and her little corner was empty. She'd have it all decorated by the time Hunter got back. She hoped he and Bronwyn had a great weekend together. Long weekend and her brain started racing, wondering where she and Derrick could go. Three or four days alone together. It would be amazing. No rushing off in the morning for work, and knowing one of them had to leave. Another task for her to research, though, one he didn't know about yet. She smiled as she hurried into her house, dutifully hung up her keys and yelled for George. He wandered out, looked at her and wandered back in again. Still it was nice to know he was here. Kept her from feeling alone. "You are lucky I love you," she yelled at him as she headed to the shower.

Derrick smiled as he walked in and heard the shower. He was hoping she'd be home when he got here. Not seeing Hannah in days wore him out mentally. He missed his blonde little girl. He adored the way she obeyed him, how she pouted when she knew she was getting a spanking, yet accepted it, the way she gave herself unconditionally in bed, and how she seemed to crave his rules and tasks. He'd have to work on that task thing. Finding things to task her with, knowing she was running a business and taking care of this house alone was challenging for him. He didn't want to overload her. He knew that she craved his discipline and his rules, though, made him want to please her, in the long run, if not always in the moment. He understood the difference and also knew she'd be disappointed in the long run if he wasn't strict and sometimes caused her pain in the short term.

This was the relationship he'd been looking for and wanting all his life, and he planned to make the most of it.

He didn't know if it was something she'd always wanted, or if she craved it but didn't know what it was exactly. Having found it, he hoped she wouldn't want to give it up any more than he did. Making a quick decision, he headed to the bathroom, dropping his clothes as he went. There was room for two in that shower.

She gave a thoroughly satisfying shriek of surprise as he

stepped into the bathroom. Grinning, he gave her something else to be surprised about.

Later, as they got dressed to go to dinner, he asked her, "What do you think about going away for a few days soon? I usually take a week or so off over the end of September, and that would be right before your busy season starts."

She smiled that sweet smile of hers at him, and said, "I think that would be lovely. Oddly, I was just thinking of that today."

"I love it when we are on the same page," he said. "Think about where you'd like to go."

"A task?" she asked him, looking delighted.

"Another one," he said. "How is the cooking class research coming along? Deadline is coming." He watched her apply a bit of some sort of makeup and smiled as she made a face. Why did women open their mouths to put eye makeup on? It amused him. But she looked so sweet doing it, it was hard to imagine that she had accomplished so much in her short life. No wonder she needed a little relief, someone to be strong for her and give her directions, because at work, she had to be the strong one. He could tell she liked it when he took charge and took care of her, guided her to becoming even better than the amazing woman she already was. It wasn't all about her. He liked being in charge and liked her following his rules, it made him feel strong and protective.

"Feel like seafood tonight?" he asked her. "There's a new place across town I've been wanting to try."

She slipped her sandals on, and said, "That sounds amazing. I'm starving."

"How about you reach up under that cute little skirt and pull those panties off, then get over here and over my knee so you can have dinner with a nice warm rear?" He said it as if it was a question, but it really wasn't.

"What?" He saw conflicting emotions race across her freshly made up face.

He pointed at her, and said, "You heard me. Get it done, so we can get to dinner."

She pouted and said, "I wasn't bad!"

"Never said you were. Now, do as you're told or I will consider that being bad."

He saw the conflict in her eyes, but then she lowered them and reached up under her skirt. "Off?"

"All the way off," he said, already knowing he wasn't going to allow her to wear them to dinner tonight. That would be a new experience for her, he imagined. He could already picture her squirming on her warm all but bare butt while they ate, or trying not to squirm anyway.

Hearing her little sigh of acceptance, he saw her reaching up under her dress, to pull them down, and half smiled as she tried not to flash him. They'd been naked in the shower together ten minutes ago and she knew darn well that skirt was going up in another minute, yet, she was trying not to let him see her as she pulled them down, and over her sandals. They were pretty little things, all blue and lacey, and he noticed her blushing furiously. Cute.

"Come on, let's warm that cute butt up, and go eat." He patted his lap and she took a reluctant step toward him.

"I don't want spanked," she said, and looked up at him with those big eyes.

"Sure you do. Now, get over here before I count to three," he said.

"Do not," she muttered but took another step.

"One, two..."

"All right, all right." She took another step over and stood in front of him. He pointed to his side, and she stuck her lip out and took another step over.

"Good girl," he said, and tugged on her arm. She went over his lap and he took his time adjusting her position, just so. "Put your hands flat on the floor and leave them there," he told her, pleased to see she did as she was told. She might protest her spankings but he could tell on some level she actually needed, if not wanted, them. Or craved his authority anyway. He rubbed her bottom then, lifted her blue flowered skirt slowly as she hung her head even lower as if in shame.

"Such a gorgeous ass you have," he said to her rubbing it more. "A little color will make it even better."

She whimpered so he decided to put her out of her misery and get started. One more rub and a smart slap that made her whimper again. He gave the other side some attention, but then went back to that one. He had no intention of making her cry tonight but wanted to let her enjoy the submissive feeling of letting go and surrendering to his authority after a few days apart.

Going over his knee with her bare bottom on display to him, her hands obediently on the floor, was a good start and warming her pretty little bottom was another way. He'd push her a little but he didn't want her miserable, just in the proper mind set.

"This is a little reminder to complete your tasks on time," he said, stepping up the pace now that he'd given her a little warm up.

"Ow! I will! I promise!" Her voice began to rise a little so he knew he was getting her attention. "Ow! That hurts!"

He saw no need to remind her spankings were supposed to hurt, that was part of the point of them. The other part, of course, was mind set, hers and his. She needed to submit to him and he needed her to do that. He also just really enjoyed spanking her adorable butt. Her hands left the floor a minute later, but she didn't try to block yet, so he didn't say anything. She'd be wiggling in a minute, trying to get away, which he always appreciated. He enjoyed the view and enjoyed knowing he had gotten through to her.

"Please, no more! Ow! I'm sorry!"

There, he got his wiggles as she attempted to roll off his lap, dodge his spanks. Not that it would do her any good, the spanking wasn't over until he decided it was over, but he'd be disappointed if she passively held still. He liked a little fire in his submission. Not much, but some made life more interesting. He didn't want a doormat, but a partner. A partner who said yes sir and agreed to have tasks and went over his knee for a proper paddling when he thought she deserved it. Or wanted it. Needed it. Or if he just felt like spanking. Sometimes he just got an itch and needed a cute butt over his knee and someone wiggling and protesting. He felt lucky to have found Hannah who seemed to have the need to wiggle and protest.

Her bottom was turning dark pink and her yelps were getting higher and her wiggles harder, so he decided to end it. He wasn't out for tears and she wasn't being punished, just reminded.

He gave her four much harder ones, right on her little sit spot where she would feel them the rest of the evening, then stopped. He rubbed a little bit while she caught her breath and calmed down. She moaned and he wondered if they would even make it to dinner.

They did, but a few hours later than he'd planned. "What looks good?" he asked her, smiling at her across the little booth. It was a hard-wooden bench and he noticed her wincing a few times, then smiling. He liked that. He liked it when he made her happy. For some reason, bruises on her butt and making it sore made her happy overall. He hadn't bruised her this time, it had been just a bit of a reminder spanking, a reminder of who was in charge here, but next time, he would make sure he left some lasting marks for her to look at. Women.

"Can you order for me, please?" Hannah asked him. Would he? Would he take charge that much?

"Sure, little girl. I'll make sure you eat well," he said, and she smiled and handed him her menu. Why she liked him taking care of her, she didn't know, but she did. It made her feel, well, protected and loved. Secure. She liked that feeling very much.

As they were eating a lovely lobster risotto, she twisted in her seat, then stopped and held still, not sure which one felt better. Why didn't this place have cushioned seats? Plus she felt, exposed, she guessed, even though she knew she wasn't. No one could see under her dress and it wasn't see-through and no one knew she was naked under there. But still, it was discomforting, she guessed was the word.

"Hunter just told me he was taking off for a few days," she said. "So I will be working extra until he gets back."

"Was this a surprise?" he asked her.

"Yeah, he sprung it on me as a done deal," she said, poking her dish. The first few bites were delicious, but now it felt a little rich. Hannah stabbed a piece of broccoli to clear her palate.

"Are you okay with that?" he asked and looked at her with that look that made her shiver.

"I am, actually. I was surprised but I'm happy he's found someone he's excited to go away with," she said. "But that kind of leaves me with extra hours to fill and a new guy to train. Plus we are still looking for a couple more people to hire. I was hoping to get a few more before next week so we could train them all together, but that won't happen now with him gone. He's in charge of hiring." She looked up and saw him looking at her in a way she didn't understand. Was he mad at her? Upset? About what?

"What?"

"Does he usually walk all over you like that?"

"Walk all over me? I have no idea what you are talking about." Hannah put her fork down and stared at him.

He stared back. She hated when he did that, she dropped her eyes and picked up her fork again to have something to do with her hands. Oh, and her mouth.

"I don't like that he dumps a bunch of work on you with no notice and you just take it," he said.

"Just take it? The store is important. The store is more

important than an inconvenience of working a few extra hours. It is a non-issue." She stared at him. She could submit in some areas but he would not be in charge of her work, any more than she could tell him not to work for Melinda. And he was still working for Melinda. How long did a stupid sunporch take? It wasn't her business like her work wasn't his.

"We can talk about it later," he said, and she put a forkful of lobster in her mouth not to answer back. Fine. They could talk about it later. Talk about what? Her work? He had nothing to do with her work. Maybe that is what they needed to talk about. He better not want her to not work. That was a deal breaker in her life. She worked hard for this store, she had loans! Debt. She had to work and she loved her work. Hunter taking a few days off to go out with his new girlfriend meant nothing long term. What was Hawk talking about? She decided not to worry about it. "Okay," she agreed.

"Yes, we want the triple chocolate cheesecake for dessert," he said to the waitress when she came over. Hannah opened her mouth, shut it, and squirmed on her all but bare bottom. Yeah, she could have some dessert and take the rest home to eat later. She would not fight over him wanting to get her chocolate. How stupid would that be?

However, how dare he try to tell her how to do her work? That was not going to happen. Was it? No. It wasn't. That was a discussion for another day, because if he thought he could tell her about her work, she could sure tell him about his.

Later that night, she brought it up again, though, because it kept niggling at her brain. "Hawk, can we talk?"

"When a woman tells you she wants to talk, that usually means a man did something wrong." He looked up from his laptop and smiled at her. She melted.

"No, I just wanted to let you know, it hurt my feelings when you were talking about my work and me not doing it right. I don't mind suggestions, of course, and I know you want to take care of me, but my brother and I really have a very good working relationship. I just wanted you to know he's not abusing me or overworking me or taking advantage of me. This was just a spur of the moment thing, and it really isn't an issue." She held her breath. How would he accept that? Would he be upset?

"Thanks for explaining. I'm just looking out for you."

Well, that was good to know, she thought, as he went back to whatever was so interesting on his laptop.

Chapter 6

"What do you need, Dad?" Jer sat in front of his computer and frowned. "I'm talking to my new roommate about what all we are contributing to the room."

"I need about five or six minutes." Derrick felt nervous, odd for him. Nothing set him off. Nothing bothered him but the little blonde girl he couldn't get out of his mind. What would Jer think about his new plans? Jer had always been the most important person in his life. Well, he had been, but now he would have his own life and his own important person, probably soon.

"I need to keep my job at the hardware store until I buy a few things with my employee discount," Jer scowled at his computer then glanced at his dad, Derrick assumed he was talking about things for his new room. He took a deep calming breath. He could do this.

"Jer. I will buy you a fridge. Just look at me. I need to tell you something," Derrick said in his best dad voice.

Jeremiah swiveled in his chair and looked at him, with his mom's eyes, and said, "Yes, Dad. I approve of you and Hannah. I'm fine and fine with it. Can I talk to my new roommate again now? He's on break from his work and has to go in five minutes. We have things to discuss."

Derrick felt as if he'd been put in his place. Having no idea what Jer knew or what he didn't know, or how he felt or anything, his astonishment at his son's perception surprised him. Why? He didn't know. Jer would be leaving for college in a couple months and Derrick was both elated for him and a little nervous. He'd never lived alone. Maybe he wouldn't though. Maybe Hannah would want to live with him. Who knew? He could command her to do some things but moving in together was not one of those things. Like her work, as she explained to him that she and her brother had an excellent working relationship and she was not being taken advantage of. He was happy to hear that, but still thought Hunter took advantage of her now and then. She really loved her work and her little store, though, so he decided unless it affected her health, mental or physical, he would let it go. After all, she stayed out of his work, though he knew that working for Melinda bothered her for some reason he didn't understand. He had no interest in the vain thing. She paid what he asked and on time and that was all he wanted.

"Good talk," he said. "I'm going to work."

"I'm heading out in about an hour, too," Jer said. "Dad, thanks. I love you, you know."

"Love you, too, kiddo. You are my favorite son, after all." Derrick felt a weird choking sensation in the back of his throat.

"Don't I know it," he said, and Derrick left the room. Did that count as getting his kid's blessing? Who knew? Was that even a thing? He didn't know that either. What did he know? That he wanted Hannah in his life. What else mattered, besides Jer? Not much that he could think of. Now what? He'd been thinking for the last few days about talking to Jer about Hannah before Jer went back to school. Sure, he'd dated often while Jer was growing up, but he'd never brought anyone other than one, home to meet him. That had been over ten years ago. He had yet to bring

Hannah 'home' because she and Jer worked together and already knew each other and Jer was always off doing his own thing and he didn't remember the last time he'd had dinner with Jer. The holidays were coming though. Surely there would be time in there, family time and time for Jer to realize how much Hannah meant to him before he left for college. He wasn't going to worry about it. He did have to make some plans though. He wanted a family dinner with Jer and Hannah, maybe two, before Jer moved out. He wondered if Jer had talked to his mom lately. He hoped so. He stayed out of their relationship, now that Jer was older and was capable, but he still felt protective about it. A boy needed a mom sometimes and Raine, as she called herself now, wasn't a bad person, despite what most of the people in town thought. She just wanted more than what Macintyre offered but realized that this was the best place for Jer to grow up. She had offered to take him a few times over the years and he had always turned her down. He didn't want his kid being dragged around the world with no stability. Rebecca-Raine thrived on it, and if Jer wanted to join her as an adult, that would be his choice now. Jer had a good head on his shoulders and he wasn't worrying about him.

What he did have to worry about was how long it was taking him to finish Melinda's sunporch, now a four-season room. It should have been done this time last month, but every time he made a little progress, something set him back. Sure, some was normal. City permits, a termite issue, backordered parts, a water line leak where she wanted a hot tub installed in her room, heavy rain for a week so work was stalled. All usual things that he'd accounted for. But then, there had been her total change in design, a break-in where someone had stolen supplies, special ordered supplies that had mysteriously gotten canceled and he'd had to reorder and wait on. Another time, Melinda had some kind of crisis and kept coming in and wanting to talk to him while crying on his shoulder. He'd felt bad enough for her, he'd stopped working to let her soak his shirt with her tears. Women. That had been a long few days. At this point in time, he felt firmly convinced she was stalling the work for some reason. He had no clue why she would not want the work done but she didn't for some reason. Why would she want to pay him to just hang around? It made no sense but then women often didn't, so there was that. He wanted to be done with it, well before his upcoming vacation so he could take Hannah somewhere she'd like to go. He had a few places in mind, but finding out what she liked was important.

Did she like to camp? Crave the ocean? Resort hotel? Whale watching? Disney? Hiking in the Shawnee National Forest, which was one of his favorite places to go, but this vacation was about her. The cooking class was about him. He could cook, of course, and could man a mean grill, and had gotten very good at yeast breads, but he didn't really enjoy cooking full meals and why have a sub if you couldn't assign her tasks you didn't want to do. He liked to eat. She needed to learn to cook.

His sub? Was she his sub? He laughed and headed out the door to work. Well, if she was, he wasn't going to be the one to tell her that, unless she was bare assed over his knee and begging. Then he might bring it up. Or not.

He picked up his phone and called her on the way to his truck, "Hey, little girl, just a quick call to let you know I'm thinking of you." He hung up and got in his truck to go to work.

Hannah smiled as she listened to his message. She loved his short little messages throughout the day but really liked them more when he gave her a task to do. Like send him a selfie or show him a picture of what she was doing, or hold up a card with a sign or something while she was at work. He kept teasing her about more things he would be requiring of her soon and she couldn't wait. Especially if she was off work and had the time to put some effort into the tasks.

"Morning, Rodney," she said, walking in the door. "How are things going?"

"Thought the boss man was coming in," he said, looking up from the register he was counting.

"Boss man said he had car trouble and wouldn't be in until tomorrow," Hannah said, and rolled her eyes. Yeah, car trouble wasn't likely. What was likely was that he and Bronwyn decided to stay an extra day on vacation. Which was fine, she could handle things here.

"Likely story," Rodney said. "Glad they are having a good time, though. Your coffee drinkers are running out of their supply. Did you get it on order yet?"

"Should be in tomorrow," she said. If that was the worst thing that happened today, it would be a good day. "Where's Tonya?"

"Running late. Car trouble."

"Seems to be going around today," she laughed and went to stash her keys and purse in her locker.

"Least it isn't the blue flu," he said. "How do you think Joseph is working out?"

"Good, so far," she said. "I'm closing with him tonight."

"You have a long day," he said. "Should have come in a little later."

"Got a lot to do," she said. Hannah didn't mind working long days at her beloved store. Some days, all she wanted was to be with Derrick, but today she knew he was out of town picking up some supplies that hadn't managed to make it to Melinda's sunporch. Then he would go to work and she would see him either tomorrow or the next day. She would start her online cooking class in a few days, called basic meal planning and preparation. Over the course of the next eight weeks, she'd be learning about nutrition and the very basics of cooking. She already knew the very basics, didn't everyone? So hopefully it wouldn't be too challenging or take up too much time. The holidays were coming fast. Today she planned to set up for fall, in a couple weeks she'd add Halloween, then the first of November, it was Christmas for two months. Loving working retail during the holidays made her weird, she knew.

Right now, she'd work the store with Rodney until Tonya and Jer showed up and then would open her packages that had arrived a few days ago, with all her yummy fall decor and get busy. It would be a fun day!

"Hey, Joseph, can you grab the other end of this?" she asked after the store closed for the night. She'd been busy all day with customers and restocking shelves, paperwork and didn't get done what she wanted done, so decided to stay later and see what all she could finish. Joseph had said he'd stay and help out. "So how's your dad doing?" she asked him.

"He's doing better since I'm here, making sure he's eating right and taking his meds on time," he said.

"You a good cook?" Hannah asked him.

"Not bad, my mom taught me, and she was a great cook. How about you?

"I suck at it. I hung out at the hardware store more than the kitchen," she said. "My boyfriend asked me to take a cooking class actually." Hannah realized that was the first time she'd said boyfriend out loud to someone. Well, he was. Nothing wrong with saying it, was there?

Joseph laughed. "Because he's too busy and important to take it?"

Hannah laughed, too. "Who knows what the man thinks." She felt a little unease. Sure, she was okay, more than okay with their relationship and craved his authority. She didn't mind, she loved doing the tasks assigned to her. But she knew other people would think it was weird. And if anyone knew he spanked her, they would think she was nuts for staying with him. Was she? Who cared? She felt happier than she ever had in her life. She loved living in Macintyre. She loved her little store and her adorable little house. She also adored and was more than likely falling in love with Derrick Hawk. What could go wrong?

"So you have a boyfriend, huh?" Joseph was saying.

"I do, and I'm very happy with him," she said. "Why? Just curious?"

"Just don't know anyone in town," he said. "Looking for a little social life."

"Hmm," she said. "Well, I haven't been here long either, but I have friends who grew up here. We'll see what we can do to make your life a little less lonely."

"When did you move here?" he asked.

"Late spring," she said. "Just bought the cutest little house and have hardly had time to fix it up any. Probably won't have time until after the holidays either."

"Retail at Christmas," he agreed. "Crazy but fun."

"I agree. Hawk tells me that Macintyre is all about Christmas. They have a night parade and everyone decorates, there are town parties, people actually go caroling. Someone brings their horse and sleigh and they do sleigh rides for the kids."

It sounded magical. She couldn't wait.

"Sounds like overkill to me," Joseph said.

"You not a Christmas person?" she asked.

"Not really. I just get through it most of the time. Did you get that?"

"Yes, got it. There. All done. You can go ahead and head home. I'll lock the door behind you."

"Sure? I can stay longer," he offered.

"I'm done paying you for the day," she said, playfully. "Out, boy!"

"Yes, ma'am," he saluted and she giggled as she walked him to the door. "See you tomorrow."

"I'll be here," he said.

What would it be like to be with someone like him, she wondered as she counted the registers in the back room.

Someone who didn't set her tasks and didn't spank her? She didn't like being spanked, except for the part where she craved them. However they always hurt way more than she thought they should. He needed to not spank as hard, she thought. He'd even mentioned using a paddle at some point! That hairbrush that one time had been hell, she didn't want anything like that again. Wondering what it might look and feel like did not count as wanting it.

They had a great time together though. They laughed and teased and she beat him in chess, and they liked the same ball team—Cardinals all the way—and he promised to take her to a game next season. Her tasks, well, she enjoyed doing those too. She liked taking care of him when he was there and loved how he cared for her. Overall, she could not be happier in their relationship. A plain, but good man like Joseph wouldn't make her happy now that she tasted this kind of lifestyle. Was something wrong with her? Who cared? Her kinks fit Derrick's apparently, so why worry too much about it?

After refilling the registers and making change for the safe for tomorrow, she packed the other cash into a bag and filled out the deposit slip, then as her dad taught her to do, put it in the waistband of her pants and untucked her shirt to cover it. She'd drop it in the night slot at the bank and head home. Looking forward to a hot shower and early bed with George ignoring her, she locked the door behind her, and headed to the parking lot at the side of the building.

"Ma'am?" a voice called out from behind her.

"Yes?" A customer who needed something after hours? That had happened before, but they would have to come back in the morning, she'd already set the alarm.

Bam! She felt something hit her behind her head and she suddenly fell forward, stumbling and hitting her head hard on the building. Her purse, yanked from her hand, was gone before she realized it.

What had just happened? She wasn't quite certain. Had she been robbed? Had she hit her head on the car? No, the brick thing. Store. She didn't know, but did know her phone was in her pocket and dialed 911 before she even tried to stand up. Better to stay here in case they, he, whoever, was still around.

Flashing blue and red lights arrived before she found the energy to get up, but had decided she wanted to take a nap now. She really should wait until she got home, but maybe she'd shut her eyes for just a minute. A police officer showed up, kneeling beside her. "I'm Officer Cooper, what happened?"

"I was leaving my store; I think I hit my head. Oh, my purse." She clutched her side and felt a sense of relief, at least she had the daily deposit still safe. That was probably what they were after. They who? Why wasn't she thinking right?

She pulled it out, to double check. "You're okay," she told the bundle.

Officer Cooper frowned. "Are you okay? Do I need to call an ambulance? Did you hurt your head?"

"I don't think so," she said. "I think I banged my leg, and hit my head, but if you could help me up?" She reached her hand up and the officer shook her head and said, "You just stay there a minute, okay? Have you been drinking?"

Had she? No. She'd been at work. Hannah started to shake her head but that hurt, so she just held still.

"What's your name?"

"Hannah Koberline," she said, feeling a bit dizzy. "I own the hardware store here and was leaving for the night." Had she already said that?

"Just sit there a minute," the officer suggested, then said something to someone who wasn't there that Hannah couldn't understand. It could be nap time now. She shut her eyes again. "Hannah, Hannah. Look at me. Anyone I can call for you while I take the report? I don't want you driving. I've got EMTs coming to evaluate you."

"Derrick Hawk," she said without thinking. Who else? Her brother was still out of town.

"Oh, I know Derrick," she said. "I have his number in my phone. He fixed my bathroom."

"Mine, too," Hannah said, shifting her leg. Did her leg hurt? It seemed to be okay.

"He fixed yours much better than mine if he's your go to contact," the officer said, seeming to laugh. "Hey, Hawk, this is Gwen Cooper. She's okay, but Hannah had a mishap. Any chance you can come down to the hardware store?" She pocketed her phone and smiled at Hannah. "He's on his way."

"Good," Hannah said, suddenly feeling like crying. "He's nice."

"You feeling dizzy or anything?" Officer Cooper asked her. "EMTs should be here in a minute."

Shaking her head for some reason, she said, "A little. Better do that report before it gets worse." She tried to smile as Gwen reached in her car and pulled out a tablet. "Okay here we go, if you're ready."

Hannah nodded and started answering questions. It didn't take as long as she thought and she only felt relief when Hawk pulled into the parking lot. "Hey, Gwen, how's Thor?" he asked as he strode over, not sounding worried but looking that way. He was cute when he was worried. She wanted to sleep now. "Let's go home to bed," she said to him.

She didn't feel like moving and he squatted down beside her, while he talked to Officer Cooper like she wasn't even here. "What happened?"

"Sounds like those Bennett kids," she said. "They've done this twice before."

"Drug heads." He shook his head. "But they have her purse?"

"But not the deposit," Hannah inserted. Hey, she was the one involved. Someone needed to talk to her! "Or my keys." She knew how he was about her keys.

He hugged her close. "So they have her address?" Why wasn't he talking to her?

"Yes, because my ID is in my purse." Duh.

They started talking about something but she didn't quite understand the words and didn't quite understand why and suddenly her ears began buzzing. Nap time now.

And she woke up in the hospital with Hawk and Hunter at her bedside. It took her a minute to realize it, but that was where she was. She could tell by the bars on the bed. Her bed at home didn't have bars.

"This is not cool," she said, her throat hurting, wishing she had a drink. "Thirsty." Okay, being a patient had its perks because both of them jumped up to stick a straw in her mouth. Hawk got there first.

"Welcome back." Hawk looked into her eyes. He reached over and hit the call button.

"Anytime," she said after she sipped some of the best water she'd ever tasted. Then she looked at her brother, "Who is watching the store?"

"Rodney, Kevin, Tonya, Jer and Joseph," he said. "We got it, kiddo, no worries."

Why did her head hurt so bad? "I need to go home and feed George."

"Yeah, you are stuck here for a few more hours, then I will take you home," Hawk said. "I've already bought new locks for your house and I'll put them in."

"Is she awake?"

Hannah blinked a few times and looked up. Not a nurse, Officer Cooper with the biggest dog she thought she'd ever seen. Was she seeing things?

"Barely," Hawk said. "Gwen, this is Hunter, Hannah's brother. Hunter, this is Officer Cooper and her partner, Thor."

Hannah heard them exchange some words and then heard Officer Cooper say, "Hannah, you awake?"

"I am," she said, forcing her eyes open.

"We found your purse and nothing was missing unless you had more than ten bucks in there. All your ID and everything is intact and I'm returning it now for you. We made copies of everything so it doesn't have to stay with us. Derrick, I'd still change her locks, just in case and keep a watch out for a while, but honestly the Bennett boys aren't the sharpest crayons in the box and I doubt they had time to even look at her address."

"Are they in custody?" Hunter asked. "Have they done this before?"

"They are and they have," Officer Cooper said as Thor went up to Hannah.

"Hi." She looked over at Officer Cooper. "Do I call him Officer?"

"You can. Or you can call him Thor, but," she smiled, "you can call me Gwen. I hear you are friends with Jessie and Marnie. I met them when I moved to town last year."

"You have a friend here, too," Hannah said, suddenly feeling more alert, better. Her headache had almost gone and she just wanted to go home and, in what she knew was a flash of clarity, she realized setting up Joseph with Gwen seemed like an amazing idea. See how well her brain was working? "Can we keep in touch?"

"Yeah, I'll be in touch. I doubt if you will have to testify, the court system knows the Bennett boys well. Their dad is not the best and their mom died from an overdose a few years ago, but I'll let you know for sure."

"I owe you a dinner when I feel better," Hannah murmured to Officer... to Gwen. "I'm taking a cooking class."

"Well, I'll sure look forward to that," she laughed. "Come on, Thor, let's get back to work."

"I'll walk you out," Hunter said.

"Thank you, Gwen, next leaky faucet is on me," Hawk said.

"I will hold you to that," she said. She, Hunter and Thor walked out the door.

"She's nice," Hannah said. "My head hurts."

"I know, little girl, I'm going to take you home soon and put you to bed, okay? Just as soon as your IV runs out." Derrick squeezed her hand. "I'm so glad you are safe. I love you, you know."

"I love you, too," she said, and shut her eyes again. She'd be glad when her head stopped hurting. She could not be happier he was there with her.

Derrick opened the door to a group of women at the door. Jessie, Marnie, Bronwyn, Tori and Gwen were there, holding platters of food and some wrapped presents.

"We came to relieve you for a couple hours. Go home, go do something," Jessie told him. "We're coming to visit and no men allowed."

Derrick already knew the lore around town, no one messed with Jess, so he just grabbed his keys and walked out the door. He'd been there over twenty-four hours and was ready to get out of the house, but only since he knew Hannah would be well taken care of. Setting the timer on his phone, he got in his truck and headed home to change and grab some clothes.

Hannah had a bad concussion and would go back to the doctor day after tomorrow to get checked out to return to work. She was already fretting about her store, but he told her no one was irreplaceable and the store would stay open until she got back there.

He heard a ding as he started his truck and checked it, hoping Hannah was okay with all the company. It wasn't

Hannah though, it was Melinda. "Can you come by? Emergency!"

Sure, why not? He'd called her and told her he was taking a few days off but if she had a problem, he would handle it for her. Then he'd go home and change clothes.

Pulling into her drive, he wondered what the issue was this time. The woman had more problems than any one person he'd ever met. Not only with her sunroom, but with her personal life that she confided to him about too often in too much detail. He didn't need to know that much about a client. He also, because he wasn't stupid, had an inkling she was attracted to him. That happened, it had happened before and would again. Hopefully, this was a real plumbing or electrical issue and not an emotional one.

He rang the bell and she opened it before it stopped ringing. "The bathroom is soaked!" she said. "There's water everywhere! Thank you so much for coming! I just didn't know what to do!" She looked on the verge of tears. Yeah, he'd seen that before. Women got emotional over busted pipes and things, mostly, he'd come to realize, from frustration and helplessness. He blamed the parents for not teaching them some basics in life, like how to tighten a loose faucet. Which was all this was. Pipe under the sink had sprung a leak. He tightened it up and put a sealer on it, and it was fixed in less than five minutes, other than the water all over the floor, but that was her issue, not his. He needed to get back to Hannah.

"Oh thank you, Hawk," she said and threw her arms around him, enveloping him in a hug. "All I could think of was ruined floors and expensive water bills and the entire house being soaked for days, and mold everywhere."

He gave a quick squeeze and stepped back, thinking, dramatic much? But he gave her an easy smile and said, "Glad to have been able to help. I'll be back as soon as that new tile comes in to continue work on your room. You try and have a good day, Melinda."

"Well, I will if I can get my housekeeper here to clean up this mess," she said.

"Good luck."

"Thank you again, Hawk, see you soon," she called out, loudly after him as he walked to the truck.

He gave her a wave from behind and got in his truck and noticed her watching him as he drove away. She was an odd thing. She seemed to have come out all right financially in her divorce. He didn't know what she did for a living, but she was always around when he was working, so he didn't know if she worked from home or just weird hours or what. Maybe she had a rich relative who died and left her a lot of money. None of his business. While she seemed set financially, she seemed very emotionally needy.

Whatever, it didn't matter to him where she got her money as long as her checks cleared. He needed to get home, tell Jer he'd be gone a couple days, talk to him about something serious, call Hunter and have the same chat, pick up a little thing he'd ordered last week, then pack up, and head back to Hannah.

"So, how are you feeling?" Jessie asked her, as Hannah propped herself up on the pillow on the couch.

"Ready to go back to work, but the ER nurse said I had to see my doctor to get cleared before I could go back, and unfortunately, Derrick heard her say that. My appointment isn't until day after tomorrow and he's going to drive me crazy." Was he? Not really. She adored his hovering mostly, but she really wanted to get back to her store. Sure, Hunter would send her updates, but if she was going to be off a few days, she wanted to be off somewhere with Derrick instead of here on the couch. Sure, everyone loved a day or two off but that was to do daily living things, like laundry and chores and going on dates, not vegging on the couch being told no. He probably wouldn't even spank her or make love to her before the doctor said it was okay. Annoying, but she giggled at the thought of Derrick asking her doctor if it was okay for her to get a good paddling. Yeah, that would go over well.

"So you all catch me up on what's going on with your lives," she said. "I've been out of touch recently."

"Just so you know, we've always had big Halloween and Christmas parties every year, the group of us. We hope you and Hunter will be joining our group this year."

"I sure will," she said, hoping she didn't have to dress up in a costume for Halloween. Not her idea of a good time. "But I can't speak for my brother. Bronwyn has seen him much more than I have." They all looked at Bronwyn, who obligingly blushed.

"We had a great long weekend at Lake Michigan," she said. "Neither one of us wanted to come home."

"So, what did you do?" Jessie probed.

"Caught fish and motored around on the bass boat he rented, and then he took me out to dinner every night. It was a great vacation. First one I've had in years."

"Vacation sounds nice," Jessie sighed. "But with soon to be three under three, I don't think we will be going anywhere for a while." She patted her stomach.

"You know you have lots of babysitters," Tori said. "Between Marnie and I, we can handle your kiddos for a few days."

"Honestly, I don't want to leave them for more than work, yet," Jessie said. " I adore my husband and it is so much fun to just be our little family. Soon to be bigger family."

"That is so nice," Marnie said, and her voice was filled with such obvious longing Hannah wanted to hug her. Wasn't Marnie married though? She had gone back to teaching this year, after a year off with her new baby. Maybe she was having a hard time adjusting. It happened, she knew. Maybe her marriage was having issues. That happened, too, she also knew. "Nothing new with me. Victor works a lot most of the time, and he's been working a lot of overtime lately, so between teaching and the kids, there isn't much time left over. Your turn, Gwen."

Okay, then, she didn't want to talk about it. Hannah exchanged a look with Jessie. They needed to talk to her later and make sure she was okay.

"Same old. Just glad to have some friends in town. Can't believe I've only been here for a couple years now," she said.

"Gwen transferred here from South Dakota. I think she was tired of the winters," Jess told Hannah.

"That and some family issues," Gwen said. "But Thor and I love it down here in Macintyre."

"He's gorgeous," Hannah said. "Where is he now?"

"Having some downtime at home," Gwen said. "He's actually my second Thor. The first one retired a few years ago, and then passed away from bone cancer not long after that. Hard to lose a friend and a partner." Her eyes teared up and Marnie gave her a hug. "But young Thor and I have bonded well."

"A dog's worst fault is they don't live long enough," Tori said. "I can't be without my ankle biters at home. You know, because I don't clean up enough poop at work, and need to do it at home." Tori ran the daycare at the local college, Hannah knew, and doubted seriously she was in charge of diapers there, but laughed with everyone else. She liked her hardware store. No poop allowed!

"So I'm doing the Christmas party at my house this year," Jessie said. "Anyone want to volunteer to do Halloween?"

Bronwyn said, "I will! It's my favorite holiday! And I've never hosted one before!"

"And now you have help," Jessie teased her. "Make that hot boy help you. We can't wait to get to know him better!"

Hannah moaned dramatically, "I don't like hearing hot used in the same sentence as my brother, that's just icky!"

They all laughed and Jessie said, "Okay, we get it but seriously, he is. Not as hot as Mac, of course."

"You and Mac, who would have thought?" Tori said.

"Everyone," Tori, Bronwyn and Marnie chorused.

"Everyone but me," Jessie added, then told Gwen and Hannah, "Mac's sister was my best friend growing up. They were twins and I never saw Mac as boyfriend material. He was always Carly's annoying brother. Now, his best friend, Brent..." she sighed and giggled. "But I ended up with Mac, so there you go."

"Wait," Hannah said. "So you plan to name one of your kids after your childhood crush?" She knew that Jessie planned to name her twins Carly and Brent but hadn't heard the story.

Jessie laughed, "I know, right? Actually Sam is named after his dad, who died in Iraq."

"Oh, I didn't know you were married before," Hannah said. "I'm so sorry."

"No, Sam isn't biologically Mac's or mine. He's Carly's son, she had a stroke and passed a few days after he was born. Mac took Sam and I came to help after he went through four nannies in three weeks or something like that. Crap happened. We got married and both adopted Sam. Then when we found out about the twins, of course one had to be Carlene, and Mac chose Brent's name for his best friend. I doubt if he knows I ever had a crush on him." She laughed. "Weird, but true!"

"Who knows what life has in store for you?" Gwen said.

"I do," Derrick's voice came from the door. "Life says it is time to let Hannah rest."

"Hannah has rested enough to last her a month," Hannah told him, pouting.

"We get it," Jessie said. "There are some casseroles in the freezer, one from each of us, and some treats. Glad you are doing okay, Hannah."

In a flurry of goodbyes, her new friends were out the door.

"Macintyre is an amazing town," Hannah told him. "I don't think I had that many friends when I left high school. I feel so at home here."

"We call that Macintyre Magic," he said. "Something in the water, I think."

"Or the air, or something," she agreed. "But I like it."

"And I like that you found us," he said, leaning against the door and looking hotter than even her brother, which made her giggle again.

"What's funny?" he asked, with a small smile.

"Bronwyn trying to tell me my brother is hot," she said. "When we all know you are the hot one around here."

"You might be prejudiced," he said.

"I might be, or maybe it's the head injury." She held her hand dramatically to her head.

"That's probably it," he said. "I brought my suitcases."

"Suitcases as in plural?" Hannah sat up and looked at him.

"Who knows how long I might have to take care of you?" he said.

"I will be fine day after tomorrow," she informed him. "Actually, I'm fine now, but you are being a pain in the butt."

"I'll probably cause a pain in your butt for the next forty or fifty years," he said.

She fanned herself. "Why, Mr. Hawk. Are you proposing to little ol' me?"

He walked over, pulling something out of his pocket. "I might be. What would you say if I did?"

"I'd say we just met and don't know each other that well, you are old, you have a son at home, I just bought a house, and hell yes." She stared at him, eyes welling with tears. Stupid head injury.

"In that case, Hannah Koberline, would you be my wife?"

"I'll be about anything you want me to be," she said as he slipped a small ring on her finger.

"I know you will, or I'll blister your butt." He kissed her.

"Is this real or am I in the hospital still and dreaming?" she asked him.

He pulled her up into his arms and smacked her butt three times, sharply, making her squeal. "What do you think?"

"I think I love you," she said.

"I thought so. You better, because I love you, too, and always will," he said and kissed her again.

The End

Megan McCoy

Megan McCoy lives in the heartland of America, surrounded by corn, soybean fields and hot guys on tractors. At home, she's raising kids, Chinese Cresteds and poodles, training them all with a tender hand and heart, while saving her sternness for the alpha males in her books. Getting up at three in the morning to write leaves her time for a few hobbies - gardening, canning, bike riding, bread baking and taking in strays.

Don't miss these exciting books by Megan McCoy and Blushing Books!

Hometown Love series
Don't Mess with Jess
Hannah and Hawk

Her Choice series
His Firecracker
The Dilemma
The City Girl
Her Choice, Always
Her Choice Forever

South Dakota Dreams series
Stormy's Trouble
Talia's Time
Wynter's Waif
Wynter's Wife

Sailor's Search

Along Came Jones Series
Sebastian
Hank
Logan and Ronnie
Logan's Contract

Single Titles
Two Weeks of Joy
An Old-Fashioned Relationship
Hard Wired Desires
Quinn's Comeuppance

Anthologies
12 Naughty Days of Christmas 2016
12 Naughty Days of Christmas 2017

Audio-Books
An Old-Fashioned Relationship

Connect with Megan McCoy
www.meganmccoy.com

Blushing Books

Blushing Books is one of the oldest eBook publishers on the web. We've been running websites that publish spanking and BDSM related romance and erotica since 1999, and we have been selling eBooks since 2003. We hope you'll check out our hundreds of offerings at http://www.blushingbooks.com.

Milton Keynes UK
Ingram Content Group UK Ltd.
UKHW020322050424
440577UK00001B/6